Fergus Hume

The Island of Fantasy

Vol. I

Fergus Hume

The Island of Fantasy
Vol. I

ISBN/EAN: 9783337064464

Printed in Europe, USA, Canada, Australia, Japan

Cover: Foto ©Andreas Hilbeck / pixelio.de

More available books at **www.hansebooks.com**

Island of Fantasy

A Romance

By FERGUS HUME

Sorrow and weariness,
Heartache and dreariness,
None should endure;
Scale ye the mountain peak,
Vale o' the fountain seek,
There is the cure.

IN THREE VOLUMES

VOL. I.

GRIFFITH FARRAN & CO. LIMITED

NEWBERY HOUSE

39 CHARING CROSS ROAD, LONDON

TO

JOHN ADDINGTON SYMONDS.

——◆——

IT was in far distant New Zealand that I first read those of your fascinating books, which deal with the poesy of Ancient Hellas, and from such perusal gained the idea which I now expand into three volumes. Here, then, is an attempt to reconstruct in a 'terra incognita'—fitly termed 'The Island of Fantasy'—the old classic life, whereof you discourse so excellently in many delightful essays. That such a venture on the part of Justinian should end in failure is perhaps to be regretted, but the reason of such mischance lay not in the scheme itself, but rather in the hostility of Nature, averse to such a resuscitated civilisation. Nevertheless, as this catastrophe but takes place in Dreamland, I see no reason why some of our over-wealthy millionaires should not carry out the Utopian project here suggested to a successful conclusion, and thus benefit the future, if not the present, by the teaching of the past.

This scheme, however, like the Island of Fantasy itself, is yet in the clouds, and, pending its being brought down

to solid earth,—if such a miracle ever does happen,—
pray allow me to inscribe to you the ideal which is not
yet the real, in recognition of the many hours of pleasure
I owe to your charming works. Unknown to me in the
flesh, you are yet my friend in the spirit through the
medium of your poetic prose, and to you therefore, in
your Swiss fastness, do I dedicate this Utopian dream
story.

FERGUS HUME.

BLANDFORD HOUSE,
ST. JOHN'S WOOD.

PROEM

THE galley waits with straining sail unfurled,
To bear us in our dreams across the sea.
Oh, ye who weary of this modern world,
Come seek the shores of solitude with me;
The winds will waft us to serener climes,
Where Hellas smiles in her dead loveliness,
And we from slumbers sorrowful will wake
To those calm antique times,
When Beauty thrilled with joy at Youth's caress,
And Genius wrought but for the laurel's sake.

Fresh blows the gale, the wine-dark ocean smiles,
For well it knows the shores its waters lave,
Our galley threads the mazes of those isles,
Which break like blossoms from the fruitful wave;
On yonder rock the fatal Sirens sang
With blended music of pipe, voice, and lyre;
And from these depths, a rising star of joy,
Bright Aphrodite sprang,
To kindle in each frozen heart her fire,
And make more sweet the lives of maid and boy.

O Pan, I, blowing through thine hollow reeds,
Awaken strains which mock the wayward breeze,
To summon Naiads from their chilly weeds,
And Dryades from the boles of haunted trees;
Alas, alas! on no immortal ear
These sylvan strains of invitation fall,
Nor through the closeness of the osier rods
Do nymphs or satyrs peer,
But only echo answers to the call,
For Pan is dead—and with him died the gods.

Yet is the earth as lovely as of yore,
And we who phantasies record in rhyme,
Can still re-people mountain, stream, and shore,
With beings bright as those of olden time.
The gods are dead indeed! but wood and sea
Are vocal yet with voice of winds and waves.
No lonely spot by barren hills confined,
But hath its sounds of glee,
Which bring that balm the saddened spirit craves,
And thus restore the music of the mind.

With such delights thy weary soul allay,
If thou would'st drink the anodyne of peace,
Forget the fierce vexations of the day,
And for the moment let your toilings cease;
On earth's fresh fairness turn thine aching eyes,
Enjoy the coolness of health-giving winds,
The voices delicate of woodlands hear,
Which hail with wordless cries;
The summer's flowerings, and the swelling rinds
Of fruits in leafless trees when snows are near.

Oh, hither come to Nature's breast for balm,
No other medicine can solace pain.
Our spirits, steeped in her eternal calm,
Will lose that restlessness which is their bane.
The forests wave in seas of whispering green,
The salt-wet winds blow from the murmuring main.
So let us lie on Mother Nature's breast,
While silently she weaves
Her spells of coolness for the aching brain,
Which soothe to stillness all its vague unrest.

CONTENTS.

THE ISLAND OF FANTASY.

CHAPTER I.

A MIND DISEASED.

Your Eastern drugs, your spices, your perfumes,
Are all in vain ;
They cannot snatch my soul from out its glooms,
Nor soothe the brain.
My mind is dark as cycle-sealèd tombs,
And must remain
In darkness till the light of God illumes
Its black inane.

IT was eight o'clock on a still summer evening, and, the ladies having retired, two
men were lingering in a pleasant, indolent
fashion over their wine in the dining-room of
Roylands Grange. To be exact, only the elder
gentleman was paying any attention to his port, for
the young man who sat at the head of the table

stared vaguely at his empty glass, and at his equally empty plate, as if his thoughts were miles away, which was precisely the case. Youth was moody, age was cheerful, for, while the former indulged in a brown study, the latter cracked nuts and sipped wine, with a just appreciation of the excellence of each. Judging from this outward aspect of things, there was something wrong with Maurice Roylands, for if reverend age in the presentable person of Rector Carriston could be merry, there appeared to be no very feasible reason why unthinking youth should be so ineffably dreary. Yet woe was writ largely on the comely face of the young man, and he joined but listlessly in the genial conversation of his companion, which was punctuated in a very marked manner by the cracking of filberts.

Without, a magical twilight brooded over the landscape, and the chill odours of eve floated from a thousand sleeping flowers into the mellow atmosphere of the room, which was irradiated by the soft gleam of many wax candles rising white and slender from amid the pale roses adorning the dinner-table. All was pleasant, peaceful, and infinitely charming; yet Maurice Roylands, aged thirty, healthy, wealthy, and not at all bad-looking, sat moodily frowning at his untasted dessert, as though he bore the weight of the world on his shoulders.

In truth, Mr. Roylands, with the usual self-worship of latter-day youth, thought he was being very hardly treated by Destiny, as that all-powerful goddess had given him everything calculated to make a mortal happy, save the capability of being happy. This was undeniably hard, and might be called the very irony of fate, for one might as well offer a sumptuous banquet to a dyspeptic, as give a man all the means of enjoyment, without providing him with the faculty of taking advantage of such good fortune. Roylands had considerable artistic power, an income of nearly six thousand a year, a fine house, and friends in-numerable—of the summer season sort; yet he neither cared for nor valued these blessings, for the simple reason that he was heartily sick of them, one and all. He would have been happier digging a patch of ground for his daily bread, than thus idling through life on an independent income, for Ennui, twin sister of Care, had taken possession of his soul, and in the midst of all his comforts he was thoroughly unhappy.

The proverb that 'The rich are more miserable than the poor,' is but a trite one on which to preach a sermon, for did not Solomon say all that there was to be said in the matter. It were easier to write a new play on the theme of Hamlet, than to compose a novel discourse on the 'All is vanity' text; for on some subjects the final word has been said, and he who preaches thereon proclaims nothing new, but merely repeats the ideas of former orators, who in their turn doubtless reiterated the sayings of still earlier preachers, and so on back to Father Adam, to whom the wily serpent possibly delivered a sermon on the cynically wise saying illustrated so exhaustively by Solomon ben Daoud. Therefore, to remark that Maurice was miserable amid all his splendours is a plagiarism, and they who desire to study the original version for themselves must read Ecclesiastes, which gives a minute analysis of the whole question, with cruelly true comments thereon.

When Roylands ten years before had gone to London, against the desire of his father, to take up the profession—if it can be so called—of a sculptor, he was full of energy and ambition. He had fully determined to set the Thames on fire by the creation of statues worthy of Canova, to make a great name in the artistic world, to become a member of the Academy, to inaugurate a new era in the history of English sculpture; so, with all this glory before him, he turned his back on the flesh-pots of Egypt and went to dwell in the land of Bohemia. In order to bring the lad to his senses, Roylands senior refused to aid him with a shilling until he gave up the pitiful trade—in this country squire's opinion—of chipping figures out of marble. Supplies being thus stopped, Maurice suffered greatly in those artistic days for lack of an assured income ; yet, in spite of all his deprivations, he was very happy in Bohemia, until he lived down his enthusiasms. When matters came to that pass, the wine of life lost its zest for this young man, and he fell a victim to melancholia, that terrible disease for which there is rarely any cure. He lived because he did not agree with Addison's Cato regarding the virtues of self-destruction, but so far as actual dying went it mattered to him neither one way nor the other. If he had done but little good during his life, at least he had done but little harm, so, thinking he could scarcely be punished severely for such a negative existence, he was quite willing to leave this world which he found so dreary, provided the entrance into the next one was of not too painful a nature.

It is a bad thing for a young man to thus take to the pessimistic school of philosophy as exemplified by Schopenhauer, for, having nothing to look back upon, nothing to look forward to, and nothing to hold on by, the scheme of his life falls into a ruinous condition, and, being without the safety anchor of Hope, he drifts aimlessly through existence, a nuisance to himself and to every one around him. Maurice, listless and despairing, did no more work than was absolutely necessary to earn a bare subsistence, and lived his life in a semi-dreamy, semi-lethargic condition, with no very distinct idea as to what was to be the ultimate end of all this dreariness. When night fell he was then more at rest, for in sleep he found a certain amount of compensation for the woes of his waking hours. As to his modelling, he took a positive dislike to it, and for this reason improved but little in his work during the last years of his Bohemian existence. Profoundly disgusted, without any positive reason, with himself, his art, the world, and his fellow-men, Heaven only knows what would have become of him, had not an event happened which, by placing him in a new position, seemed to promise his redemption from the gloomy prison of melancholia.

The event in question was none other than the death of his father, and Maurice, as in duty bound, came down to the funeral. When the will of the late Squire was read, it was discovered that, with the exception of one or two trifling bequests, all the real and personal property was left to his only son; thus this fortunate young man at the age of thirty found himself independent of the world for the rest of his days, provided always he did not squander his paternal acres, a thing he had not the slightest intention of doing. Maurice had no leanings towards what is vulgarly termed a 'fast life,' for he detested horse-racing, cared but little for wine, and neither cards nor women possessed any fascination for him. Not that he was a model young man by any means, but his tastes were too refined, his nature too intellectual, to admit of his finding pleasure in drinking, gaming, and their concomitants. As to love, he did not know the meaning of the word,—at least not the real meaning,—which was rather a mistake, as it would certainly have given him an interest in life, and perhaps have prevented him yielding so readily to the influence of 'Black Care,' about whom even the genial Venusian knew something, seeing that he made her an equestrian.

Of course, he was sorry for the death of his father, but there had been so little real sympathy between them, that he could not absolutely look upon the event as an irreparable calamity. Maurice had always loved his mother more than his father, and when she died as he was leaving home for college he was indeed inconsolable; but he saw the remains of the late Mr. Roylands duly committed to the family vault without any violent display of grief, after which he returned to live the life of a country gentleman at the Grange, and wonder what would be the upshot of this new phase of his existence.

Solitude was abhorrent to him, as his thoughts were so miserable; therefore, for the sake of having some one to drive away the evil spirit, he invited his aunt, the Hon. Mrs. Dengelton, to stay at the Grange for a week or so. She came without hesitation, and brought her daughter Eunice also, upon which Maurice, finding two women more than one unhappy bachelor could put up with, asked the new poet Crispin, for whom he had a great liking, to come down to Roylands, which that young man did very willingly, as he was in love with Eunice, a state of things half guessed, and wholly hated by Mrs. Dengelton, who much desired her daughter to marry the new Squire.

On this special evening, the Rev. Stephen Carriston, Rector of Roylands, had come to dinner, and, Crispin having retired to the drawing-room with the ladies, he found himself alone with his former pupil, much to his satisfaction, as he wished greatly to have a quiet talk with Maurice. Mr. Carriston was the oldest friend the young man had, having been his tutor in the long ago, and prepared him for college. Whatever success Maurice gained at Oxford—and such success was not inconsiderable—was due to the admirable way in which he had been coached by the rubicund divine.

Certainly the Rector loved the good things of this life, and looked as if he did so, which is surely pardonable enough, especially in a bachelor ; for at sixty-five years of age the Rector was still single, and much beloved by his parishioners, to whom he preached short, pithy sermons on the actions of their daily lives, which was assuredly better than muddling their dull brains with theological hair-splitting. Being very fond of Maurice, he was greatly concerned to see the marked change which ten years of London life had made in the young fellow. The merry, ambitious lad, who had departed so full of resolution to succeed, had now returned a weary-looking, worn-out man ; and as the Rector, during the intervals of his nut-cracking, glanced at his former pupil, he was struck by the extreme melancholy which pervaded the whole face. Comely it was certainly, of the fresh-coloured Saxon type, but the colour had long since left those haggard cheeks, there were deep lines in the high forehead, the mouth was drawn downward in a dismal fashion under the trim moustache, and from the eyes looked forth an unhappy soul.

Yes, the Rector was considerably puzzled to account for this change, and resolved to find out what ailed the lad, but he hardly knew how to set about this delicate task, the more so, as he feared the consolations of religion would do but little good in this case; for Maurice, without being absolutely a sceptic, yet held opinions of a heterodox type, quite at variance with the declarations of the Thirty-Nine Articles in which the good Rector so firmly believed.

At length Mr. Carriston grew weary of cracking nuts and sipping port wine without the digestive aid of pleasant conversation, and therefore began to talk to his quondam pupil, with the firm determination to keep on talking until he discovered the secret of the young man's melancholy.

'Are you not going to fill your glass, Maurice?'

'No, thank you, sir. I am rather tired of port.'

'Inexplicable creature!' said the Rector, holding up his glass to the light. 'Ah, well, "*De gustibus*," my dear lad. I have no doubt you can finish the quotation. Why not try claret?'

' I'm tired of claret.'

' It seems to me, sir,' observed Mr. Carriston leisurely, ' that you are tired of all things.'

' I am—including myself.'

' Strange! A young man of thirty years of age, sound of mind and body, who is fortunate enough to inherit six thousand a year, ought to be happy.'

' Money does not bring happiness '

' Ah, that proverb is quite worn out,' replied the Rector cheerily ; ' try another, my boy, try another.'

Maurice, leaning forward with a sigh, took a handful of nuts, which he proceeded to crack in a listless fashion. The Rector said nothing, but waited for Maurice to speak, which he was obliged to do out of courtesy, although much disinclined to resume the argument.

' I've tried everything, and I'm tired of everything.'

' Even of that marble-chipping you call art ? '

' I am more tired of that than of anything else,' said Maurice emphatically.

' A bad case,' murmured the Rector, shaking his grey head ; ' a very bad case, which needs curing. " Nothing's new ! nothing's true ! and no matter," says my Oxford fine gentleman. Maurice, I must assert my privilege as an old friend, and reason with

you in this matter.   I am sadly afraid, my dear lad,
that you need whipping.'

The ghost of a smile played over the tired face of
the young man, and he assented heartily to the
observation of his old tutor—nay, even added an
amendment thereto.

'I do, sir, I do!' he said sombrely; 'we all need
whipping more or less—men, women, and children.'

'I am afraid the last-named get the most of it,'
replied Carriston, with dry humour.

'With the birch, yes.   But 'tis not so pleasant to
be whipped by Fate.'

'My dear lad, you cannot say she has whipped
you.'

'To continue your illustration, Rector, there are
several modes of whipping,—the birch which pains
the skin, poverty which pains the body, and despair
which pains the soul.   The latter is my case.   I have
health, wealth, and youth; but I feel the stings of
the rod all the same.'

'Yes?' queried Carriston interrogatively; 'in what
way?'

'I have not the capability of enjoying the blessings
I possess.'

'How so?   Explain this riddle.'

' I cannot explain it. I simply take no pleasure in life. Rich or poor, old or young, well or ill, I should still be as miserable as I am now.'

' Hum! Let us look at the question from three points of view—comprehensive points. The legal, the medicinal, the religious. One of these, if properly applied, will surely solve the enigma.'

' I doubt it.'

' Ah, that is because you have made up your mind to doubt. "None so blind as those who won't see."'

' Who is quoting proverbs now, Mr. Carriston?'

' I am, sir, even I who dislike such arid chips of wisdom ; but 'tis an excellent proverb, which has borne the wear and tear of centuries. Come now, Maurice, are you in any trouble connected with money? are you involved in any law-suit, or—or— well,' said the Rector, delicately eyeing his glass, 'I hardly know how to put it,—er—er—are you involved in any love affair?'

' No ; my worldly position is all right, and I am not mixed up in any feminine trouble.'

' Good ! that settles the legal point. Now for the medical. Your liver must be out of order.'

' I assure you, sir, I never felt better in my life.'

Mr. Carriston's face now assumed a grave expression as he put the last question to his host.

'And the religious point?'

'I am not troubled on that score, sir.'

The Rev. Stephen looked doubtful.

'Whatever my religious views may be,' resumed Maurice, seeing the Rector was but half convinced, 'and I am afraid they can hardly be called orthodox, I at least can safely say that my past life is not open to misconstruction.'

'Good! good! I always had confidence in you, Maurice. Yours is not the nature to find pleasure in gutter-raking. Well, it seems that none of those three points meet the case. Can you not give me some understandable reason for this melancholy which renders your life so bitter.'

'No. I went to London full of joy, energy, and ambition; but in some way—I cannot tell you how—I lost all those feelings. First joy departed, then ambition fled away, and with these two feelings absent I felt no further energy to do anything. It may be satiety, certainly. I have explored the heights and depths of London life, I have read books new and old, I have studied, so far as in me lay, my fellow-men, I have tried to fall in love with my fellow-women—and failed dismally. In fact, Mr. Carriston, I have exhausted the world, and find it as empty as this.'

He held up a nut which he had just cracked, and it contained no kernel—an apt illustration of his wasted life.

The Rector shook his head again in some perplexity, and filled himself another glass of port, while Maurice, rising from his seat, sauntered to the window, and looked absently at the peaceful scene before him. The moon, rising slowly over the tree-tops, flooded the landscape with her pale gleam, so that the gazer could see the glimmer of the white marble statues far down in the dewy darkness of the lawn, the sombre woods black against the clear sky, and away in the distance the thin streak of silver, which told of the restless ocean. A salt wind was blowing overland from thence, and, dilating his nostrils, opening his mouth, he inhaled the vivifying breeze in long breaths, while dully in his ears sounded the sullen thunder of the far-away billows rolling landward in sheets of shattered foam.

'Oh, Mother Nature! Demeter! Tellus! Isis!' he murmured, half closing his eyes; ''tis only from thee I can hope to gain a panacea for this gnawing pain of life. I am weary of the world, tired of this aimless existence, but to thee will I fly to seek solace in thy healing balms.'

'Maurice!'

'Yes, sir.'

It was the Rector who spoke, and the sound of his mellow voice roused the young man from his dreaming; therefore, resuming his normal manner, he lighted a cigarette and prepared to listen to the conversation of his old tutor.

'Are you still as good a German scholar as you used to be?' asked the Rector deliberately.

'Not quite. My German, like myself, has grown somewhat rusty.'

'Can you translate the word *Selbstschenerz?*'

'Self-sickness.'

'Yes; that is about as good an English equivalent as can be found. Well, that is what you are suffering from.'

'Oh, wise physician,' retorted Roylands, with irony. 'I know the cause of the disease myself, but what of the cure?'

'You must fall in love.'

'No one can fall in love to order.'

'Well, you must make the attempt at all events,'

said Carriston, with a genial laugh; 'it is the only cure for your disease.'

'Why do you think so?'

'Because 'tis your egotism makes you miserable. You care for no one but yourself, and are therefore bound to suffer from such selfishness. True happiness lies in self-abnegation, a virtue which all men preach, but few men practise. "Every man," says Goethe, "thinks himself the centre of the universe." This is true—particularly true in your case. You have been so much taken up with your own woes and troubles that you have had no time to see those of your fellow-creatures, and such exclusive analysis of one's inner life leads naturally to self-sickness. You are torturing yourself by yourself; you have destroyed the sense of pleasure, and can therefore see nothing good on God's earth. You would like to cut the Gordian knot by death, but have neither the courage nor the resolution to make away with yourself. Oh, I know the reason of such hesitation.

'*Tis better to endure the ills we have,*
Than fly to others that we know not of.

I have no doubt that is your feeling about the hereafter. Well, with all this you feel you are in a prison and cannot escape, because a last remnant of manliness forbids you opening the only door by which you can go hence. Therefore you are forced to remain on earth, and are condemned yourself to supply the tortures from which you suffer. Have I not described your condition accurately?'

'You have,' replied Maurice, rather astonished at the Rector's penetration. 'I do torture myself, I know, but that is because I cannot escape from my own thoughts. Pin-pricks hurt more than cannon balls, and incessant worries are far more painful than great calamities. But all you have said touches on the disease only, it does not say how the cure you propose will benefit me.'

He had come back to his seat, and was now leaning forward with folded arms, looking at the benevolent face of his friend. The discussion, having roused his interest, made him forget himself for the moment, and with such forgetfulness the moody look passed away from his face. The Rector saw this, and immediately made use of it as a point in his favour.

'Ah, if you could but behold yourself in the glass at this moment,' he said approvingly, 'you would see the point I am aiming at without need of further discussion. I have interested you, and consequently you have forgotten for the moment your self-torture. That is what love will do. If you love a woman, she will fill your whole soul, your whole being, and give you an interest in life. What she admires you will admire, what she takes an interest in, you will take an interest in ; and thus, being busy with other things, you will forget to worry your brains about your own perfections or imperfections. And if you are happy enough to become a father, children will give you a great interest in life, and you will find that God has appointed you work to do which is ready to your hand. When you discover such work, aided by wife and children, you will do it, and thus be happy. Remember those fine words of Burns—

> *To make a happy fireside clime*
> *For weans and wife,*
> *That's the true pathos and sublime*
> *Of human life.'*

'What you say sounds fine but dull. I don't care about such wearisome domesticity.'

'What you call wearisome domesticity,' said the Rector in a voice of emotion, 'is the happiest state in which a man can find himself. Home, wife, children, domestic love, domestic consolations—what more can the heart of man desire? Laurel crowns

cure no aching head, but the gentle kiss of a loved
wife in time of trouble is indeed balm in Gilead.'

Maurice looked at the old man in amazement, for
never had he seen him so moved.

'You speak feelingly, Rector,' he said at length,
with a certain hesitation.

'I speak as I feel,' replied Carriston, with a sigh.
'I also have my story, old and unromantic-looking as
I am.   Come over to the Rectory to-morrow, my dear
lad, and I will tell you something which will make
you see how foolish it is to be miserable in God's
beautiful world.'

'I'm afraid it will give you pain.'

'No ; it will not give me pain.   What was my
greatest sorrow is now my greatest consolation.   You
will come and see me to-morrow?'

'If you wish it.'

'I do wish it.'

'Then I will come.'

There was silence for a few moments, each of them
being occupied with his own thoughts.   The Rector
was evidently thinking of that old romance which had
stirred him to such an unwonted display of emotion ;
and Maurice saw for the first time in his selfish life
that other men had sorrows as well as he, and that he

was not the only person in the world who suffered from *Selbstschmerz*.

'But come, Maurice,' said the Rector, after a pause, 'I was talking about curing you by marriage.'

'Love!'

'Well, marriage in your case, I hope, will be love,' observed Carriston, a trifle reproachfully. 'I would be sorry indeed to see you make any woman your wife unless it was for true love's sake.'

'Well, whom do you wish me to love?'

'Ah, that is for you to decide. But, if I may make a suggestion, I should say Eunice.'

'Eunice!'

'She is a charming girl. Highly educated, good-looking'—

'But so prim.'

'Oh, that is but a suspicion of old-maidism, which will wear off after a month or two of married life.'

'Do you think she would make me a good wife?'

'I am sure of it.'

'So am I,' said Maurice, with a faint sneer. 'She would look well at the head of my table; she would always be dressed to perfection; she would doubtless be an excellent mother; but there is one great bar to our union.'

' And that is ? '

' We only love each other as cousins.'

' It may grow into a warmer feeling.'

' I'm certain it won't ; and, Rector,' continued
Maurice, laying his hand on the old man's arm, ' could
you advise me to have a mother-in-law like Mrs.
Dengelton ? '

The Rector laughed heartily, and Maurice joined
in his mirth, much to Carriston's delight.

' Ah, now you are more like the boy I knew !' he
said, slipping his arm into that of Roylands, and
leading him to the door ; ' did I not tell you I would
cure you ?   I will complete the cure to-morrow.'

' But it might give you pain.'

' No, no; don't think about that,' said Carriston
hastily. ' If I can do you a service, I don't mind a
passing twinge of regret. But here we are at the
drawing-room door.   Let us join the ladies.'

' And Crispin.'

' By the way,' said the Rector, placing his hand on
Roylands as he was about to open the door, ' who is
Crispin ? '

' Every one in London has been trying to find that
out for the last two years.'

' What is he ? '

'The new poet; the coming Tennyson, the future Browning. No one knows who he is, or where he comes from. He is called Crispin *tout court.*'

'A most perplexing person. Are you quite sure'—

'If he is fit for respectable society? Oh yes. He goes everywhere in London. Like Disraeli, he stands on his head, for his genius—and he has great genius—has opened to him all the drawing-rooms of Belgravia. I assure you, he is quite proper.'

'Still, still!' objected the Rector.

'Well, what objection have you yet to him, my dear sir?'

'I'm afraid, I'm afraid,' whispered Carriston, looking apprehensively at Maurice, 'that he loves Eunice.'

'Impossible!'

'Oh, I'm not so old but what I can see the signs and tokens of love; and, placed on my guard by a casual glance, I noticed Eunice and your poet particularly at dinner.'

'In that case,' said Maurice coolly, 'I'm afraid Crispin will have to put up with Mrs. Dengelton as a mother-in-law.'

The Rector laughed again, and they entered the drawing-room.

CHAPTER II.

DE RERUM PARVULA.

The smallest actions in a life
Betray the calm or inward strife:
From idle straws, as persons know,
One learns the way the breezes blow;
You love those Florentine mosaics,
Yet tiny stones the picture makes.
Complying with this rule's demand,
Whate'er is meant you'll understand;
So follow carefully this chatter,
And you'll discover what's the matter.

HE three persons who occupied the drawing-room were each employed according to their different natures, for Crispin, being an ardent musician, was seated at the piano, playing softly; Eunice, who rarely spoke, was listening; and the Hon. Mrs. Dengelton was talking—as usual. She was always talking, but never by any chance said anything worth hearing. With her it was all quantity and no quality; for, wherever she was,

in drawing - room, theatre, or park, her sharp
strident voice could be heard above all else. Certainly she was silent in church, but it must have
been an effort for her to hold her tongue, and
she fully made up for it when outside the door, by
chattering all the way home. Scandal said she had
talked her husband dead and her daughter silent ;
and certainly the Hon. Guy Dengelton was safe in
the family vault, while Eunice, as a rule, said very
little. Mrs. Dengelton knew every one and everything, and, had it been the fashion to write memoirs,
after the mode of the eighteenth century, she could
have produced a book which would have made a
sensation, and which would have been suppressed—
after the first edition. Owing to her incessant stream
of small talk, she was known in society as 'The Parrot,'
a name which exactly fitted her, as she had a hook
nose, beady eyes, and was always dressed in gay
colours. Add to this description her *esprit*, as she
called it, but which scandal said was French for the
vulgar American word 'jaw,' and you have a faithful
portrait of the most dreaded woman in London.

Reasons ? two ! She knew stories about every one,
which she retailed to their friends at the pitch of her
voice ; and she was always hunting for a husband

for Eunice. Eldest sons had a horror of her, and
the announcement that Mrs. Dengelton was to be at
any special ball was sufficient to keep all the eligible
young men away. Consequently, no one asked 'The
Parrot' to a dance unless the invitation was dragged
out of them ; but Mrs. Dengelton was skilful at such
work, and went about a good deal during the season.
Hitherto she had not been successful in her husband-
hunting, as no one would marry Eunice, with the
chance of having Mrs. Dengelton as mother-in-law.
Crispin certainly was daring enough to pay his
addresses, but Crispin had neither name, title, nor
family, nothing but his genius, and Mrs. Dengelton
therefore frowned on his suit. When Maurice came
in for the Roylands estate, his aunt thought it was
desirable for Eunice to marry her first cousin, 'just
to keep the property in the family,' as Mrs. Dengelton
put it, though how such a saying applied in this case
it is rather difficult to see. However, The Parrot
gladly accepted her nephew's invitation,—when she
arrived, he regretted having asked her, — and came
down with Eunice, with the firm determination to talk
Maurice into matrimony.

She was very angry when Crispin arrived, and
forbade Eunice to encourage the young man, but

she could scarcely turn him out of the house, as she would have liked to have done, so she put up with his presence as best she could, and never lost an opportunity of saying disagreeable things to him in a covert fashion.

Eunice herself was a charmingly pretty girl, who very much resented the way in which her mother put her up to auction, but, being rather weak-willed, could not combat Mrs. Dengelton's determination, and submitted quietly to be dragged about all over the place, with the hope that some day a modern St. George would deliver her from this dragon.

St. George, long looked for, unexpectedly appeared one day in the person of Crispin, and, though Mrs. Dengelton laughed at the idea of her daughter throwing herself away on a pauper, Eunice, nevertheless, fell in love with the poet. Crispin would have married her at once, but, in spite of her anxiety to get beyond the clack of Mrs. Dengelton's tongue, she was too much afraid of that strong-willed lady to break out into open mutiny, so poor St. George had to adore her in secret, lest the dragon should pounce down on him.

Crispin! who ever heard of such a name? being the more singular as it had neither head nor tail.

If he had been Henry Crispin, or Crispin Jones,
people could have put up with the oddness of the
sound; but Crispin, alone, sounded heathenish, to
say the least of it. No one knew who Crispin was,
nor where he came from, for he had, two years
previous, suddenly flashed like a meteor upon literary
London with a book of brilliant poems, which made
a great success. For once the critics were unani-
mous in praising good work, and pronounced 'The
Roses of Shiraz, and Other Poems' to be the
finest series of poetical Eastern tales since Lord
Byron had enchanted the world with 'The Giaour'
and 'The Bride of Abydos.' For the critics' praise or
blame Crispin seemed to care but little, nor did he
satisfy the curiosity of those up-to-date people who
desired to meet him. Sometimes he would appear in
a Belgravian drawing-room, but only for a moment,
and would then leave England for a tour in his
beloved East. Just when the world would begin to
forget him, he would suddenly reappear in society,
and fascinate one and all by his charming manners.
Handsome he was not, being small and dark, but he
was as lithe as a serpent, and his dark eyes flashed
with the wondrous light of genius. All sorts of stories
were told about him, and none of them were correct,

though Mrs. Dengelton was ready to swear to the truth of at least half a dozen. In fact, he puzzled society very much, and, as society always takes to that which it cannot understand, Crispin was quite the lion of the season.

An article entitled 'The Lord Byron of our days' appeared in a leading society paper, which retailed wonders about this unknown poet; but Crispin neither contradicted nor affirmed the truth of these statements, therefore became more of a puzzle than ever. He was a brilliant musician; he spoke several languages, and seemed to have been all over the world; but beyond this he was a mystery. To no one, not excepting Maurice, who was his closest friend, did he tell the story of his life, and even Mrs. Dengelton, who was an adept at finding out things people did not want known, could make nothing of him.

Then Crispin met Eunice, and all his heart went out to this dainty, dark-haired girl, who spoke so seldom, but whose eyes and gestures were so eloquent. "The Fairy of Midnight,' he called her, and often wondered how such a woman as Mrs. Dengelton ever came to have so silent and lovely a daughter. To Crispin, steeped in the lore of the East, she was like a Peri, and her love inspired him with exquisite

love poems, some of which appeared in *The Nineteenth Century* and *The Fortnightly Review.* Whether
he told her who he was is doubtful—if he did, Eunice
never betrayed his confidence, for she was a woman
who could keep a secret, which was a miracle, seeing
her mother was such a gossip.   They loved and
suffered in silence with such discretion, that even
keen-eyed Mrs. Dengelton did not guess the understanding which existed between them, and was hard
at work trying to arrange a marriage with Maurice,
quite unaware that her meek daughter had made up
her mind to marry no one but this mysterious
Crispin.

Sitting at the piano, Crispin was playing a sensuous
Eastern air with the soft pedal down, and looking at
Eunice, whose eyes responded eloquently to his
glances.   Neither of them paid much attention to
the chatter of The Parrot, who was quite ignorant of
the love-making going on under her nose, for both
Eunice and Crispin had arrived at the stage of complete union of souls which renders words superfluous
while eyes can talk.

Mrs. Dengelton was 'doing' a parrot in beadwork
for a screen, and the gaudy bird might have passed
for her portrait, so like her did it seem.   Luckily, the

beadwork parrot could not talk, but its creator could, and did with as few pauses as possible.

'As I was saying, my dear Eunice, there is something very strange about this silence of my dear nephew. I've no doubt it is smoking too much,—so many young men smoke in that dreadful place, Bloomsbury, where he lived,—or perhaps he feels a little out of society after living so long away from it. Oh, I know Bloomsbury! yes! I sometimes visit the poor there. How strange I never came across poor dear Maurice! He is so sadly altered, not gay like he used to be. I do not really think he knows how to laugh, and '—

At this moment, as if to give the lie to Mrs. Dengelton's assertion, her nephew entered the room, laughing, in company with the Rector; but the good lady did not know that she was the cause of this hilarity, and at once began to deluge the new-comers with the fountain of her small talk.

'Now, my dear Rector and my dear Maurice, what are you laughing at? Is it some amusing joke? Oh, I am sure it is! Eunice, Mr. Crispin, we are going to be told something funny '—

'But really, my dear lady,' began the Rector, with uplifted hand, ' I '—

'Now you need not tell me it is not funny, because it has made Maurice laugh, and he has been as grave as a judge since we came down. I was just saying to Eunice when you came in'—

'My dear aunt, the joke is not worth telling you,' said Maurice, in desperation cutting her short.

'Ah, I knew there was a joke! Do tell it to Eunice! she is so fond of amusing stories, especially from you.'

Maurice flushed angrily.

'I don't tell amusing stories,' he said curtly, and walked across to the piano.

'Such a bad temper!' sighed The Parrot, shaking her head; 'so like his poor dear father, who foamed at the mouth when in a rage.'

'Oh, come, not so bad as that,' said the Rector good-naturedly.

'My dear Rector, I assure you I have seen Austin'— And then Mrs. Dengelton began a long, rambling story, which had no beginning, and certainly did not appear to have an end, for she droned on until the poor Rector, quite weary, was much put to, to conceal his yawns.

Meanwhile, Maurice, remembering what the Rector

had told him about the young couple, looked keenly at the poet and then at his cousin, at which inspection they naturally felt somewhat embarrassed.

'Yes?' said Eunice at length, in an interrogative fashion.

'Oh, nothing, nothing!' he responded hastily; 'I was only wondering what you were talking about.'

'We were not talking at all,' said Crispin, running his fingers over the keys; 'on the contrary, we were listening to Mrs. Dengelton.'

Maurice smiled absently, and tugged moodily at his moustache.

'You have a charming place here, Roylands,' remarked Crispin, more for the sake of saying something than for the importance of the remark; 'I would like to settle down in this quiet village.'

'You!' said Maurice in astonishment; 'the bird of passage who is never off the wing! Why, you would die of ennui in a week.'

'Ah, that depends on the company,' answered Crispin, stealing a glance at Eunice, who sat silently playing with her fan.

'I am afraid I am not very lively company,' observed Maurice, with a sigh, not noticing the glance; 'there is so little to talk about now-a-days.'

' Poetry.'

' I'm tired of poetry.'

' Music.'

' Too much music is dreary.   I heard such a lot in London.'

' Then you must love scandal.'

' Ah, that is a hint that my dear aunt can amuse me.'

' Maurice !' said Eunice, with a frown.

' Now don't be angry, my dear cousin.   Talking scandal is a very harmless occupation, and, as the Rector seems interested, I think I will go and hear the latest story of Belgravia.   But, Crispin, I wish you would take my cousin on to the terrace—the sky is worth looking at with moon and clouds.'

Crispin darted a look of gratitude at him, and Maurice, delighted at thus foiling his aunt's schemes, went off to hear that lady's conversation.

The two lovers at the piano were afraid to move for a time, lest they should attract Mrs. Dengelton's attention, and thus be prevented from leaving the room ; but when they saw her deep in conversation with the two gentlemen, they stole quietly to the French window at the end of the room, through which they speedily gained the terrace.

'Do you feel cold, Eunice?' asked Crispin, noticing his companion shiver.

'A little.'

'Wait a moment, then. Your mother left a shawl near the window, I'll fetch it to you at once.'

'Take care she does not see you.'

'Not much fear of that ; she has an audience, and is happy.'

He went off laughing quietly ; and Eunice, leaning on the balustrade of the terrace, stared at the wonderful beauty of the sky. Away in the west shone the silver round of the moon, and below her were gigantic black clouds, the edges of which were tipped with light. They looked like colossal rocks piled up from earth to heaven, and above them shone the serene planet in an expanse of blue, as if she scorned their efforts to veil her face. Far below Eunice heard the musical splash of the fountains, and the chill odours of flowers floated upward, as though drawn by the spell of her beauty. She looked wonderfully lovely with her delicate face turned upward to the moon, and so thought Crispin, as he came lightly along the terrace with the fleecy shawl over his arm.

'I shall no longer call you the Fairy of Midnight,'

he whispered, wrapping the shawl round her shoulders ;
' your name will be the " Moon Elf." '

' Ah, what a charming title for a fairy story ! ' said
Eunice, who was anything but silent when away
from her mother. ' Why do you not write a fairy
story ? '

' Because I am living one now.'

' Flatterer ! '

' No ; I am speaking the truth. I adore a lovely
princess, who is guarded by an elderly dragon breathing the fire of scandal '—

' You must not talk of my mother like that.'

' Then I will not. She is the most charming lady
I know.'

' Oh ! '

' What ! you are not pleased at that ? My dearest
Eunice, how cruel you are ! But indeed I do not
love your mother. She will not let me marry you.'

' No ; she wants me to marry Maurice,' said Eunice,
with a sigh.

' I am afraid that ambition will never be gratified.
Maurice is our friend.'

' Do you think he knows we love one another ? '

' I am sure he does. But he knows to-night for the
first time ; I saw it in his eyes when he looked at us.'

' How can he have guessed ? '

' He did not guess. No ; Roylands has never been in love, and only a lover can recognise the silent eloquence of love. But I think that keen-eyed old Rector '—

' What ! Mr. Carriston ? Impossible ! How could he tell we loved one another ? '

' Well, going by the theory I have propounded, he must have at one time of his life been in love himself, and therefore intuitively guessed our hidden romance.'

' But he is a bachelor.'

' Ah, then he has had a romance also ! An extinct volcano perhaps.'

' And Maurice ? '

' Is not a volcano at all—at least, not so far as I know. He has never been in love yet, but he will be some day.'

' When ? '

' Pardon me, I cannot lift the veil of the future. But I admit Maurice with his melancholia puzzles me.'

' Well, you puzzle every one yourself. They call you the riddle of London.'

' I will explain my riddle self to you when we marry.'

'I am afraid that will never be.'

'Indeed it will,' he said gaily. 'But you need not be afraid of my mystery; I have no Bluebeard chamber to keep locked, I assure you. Do you hesitate to marry me on account of my so-called mystery?'

'No; I trust you too much for that.'

'My dearest!'

At this moment the moon veiled her face discreetly behind a wandering cloud, and their lips met in a kiss—a kiss of pure and enduring love. Then Crispin tenderly wrapped the shawl closer round the shoulders of Eunice, and arm in arm they strolled up and down the terrace, talking of their present despairs, their future hopes, and their possible marriage.

Meanwhile, Mrs. Dengelton, quite unaware of the way in which all her matrimonial schemes were being baffled by this audacious poet, was holding forth to Maurice and the Rector on the subject of a family romance. For once in her life she proved interesting, for Maurice only knew the skeleton of Roylands by name, and was quite unaware of the reason it was locked up in the cupboard. It was wonderful what a lot of good the conversation of the

Rector had done him, and now, having been once
roused out of his melancholia, he was quite interested
by the tale which his aunt was telling. The Rev.
Stephen Carriston noticed the bright look on his
usually sad face, and was delighted thereat.

'I will complete the cure to-morrow,' he repeated
to himself; and then prepared to listen to Mrs.
Dengelton's story, which interested him very much,
the more so as he knew the principal actors concerned
therein.

'Of course I only speak from hearsay, my dear
Rector,' she said, laying aside her beadwork so as
to give her eloquence every chance; 'at the time
these events took place I was just a baby in long
clothes. You, Rector, perhaps know the story better
than I do.'

'No; I had just left college when Rudolph
Roylands ran away, but I knew him at the univer-
sity.'

'Ah yes; of course. You were very friendly with
both my brothers, I believe, so it is curious they
never told you of their love for Rose Silverton.'

'Well—I heard something about it,' said the
Rector, with a hesitating glance at Maurice.

'Oh, my dear Rector, I am going to say nothing

against my sister-in-law! She was a very charming woman.'

'She was all that was good and pure,' remarked Maurice abruptly; annoyed, he knew not why, at the tone adopted by Mrs. Dengelton in speaking of his dead mother.

'Yes, I know she was. Still, my dear Maurice, you must pardon my plain speech, but she did flirt terribly with Rudolph.'

'My lost uncle? Ridiculous!'

'It is not ridiculous at all,' said the lady, drawing herself up; 'it was on your mother's account Rudolph left England.'

'Who said so?' demanded Maurice indignantly.

'Every one; even your father.'

Maurice was about to make some remark, when he caught sight of a warning look on Carriston's face, therefore held his peace.

'What I was about to remark,' pursued Mrs. Dengelton, choosing her words carefully, 'was, that, when my brothers, Rudolph and Austin, came home, —the first from his regiment, the second from college,—they both fell in love with Rose Silverton, whose father was a retired captain in the army. Rudolph, as you know, Rector, was the heir to

Roylands, and Captain Silverton naturally wanted Rose to marry him, as the match was such a good one. She, however, preferred Austin.'

'Love *versus* Money, and Love was triumphant,' said Maurice, smiling.

'If you put it like that, I suppose it was,' replied his aunt frigidly. 'Well, Rose, as I have said, flirted considerably with Rudolph, though she loved my brother Austin best. Oh, you need not shake your head, Rector—Rose did flirt!'

'My dear aunt, spare the dead,' observed Maurice, with a groan, for this old lady was really terrible with her malignant tongue.

'I hope I am too good a churchwoman to speak evil of any one, dead or alive,' said Mrs. Dengelton, with dignity. 'But I will make no further remarks if they are so displeasing to you, though why they should be displeasing I cannot conceive. Well, to gratify her father, Rose appeared to favour Rudolph, but in secret she met Austin. Such duplicity! I beg your pardon, Maurice, but it was duplicity.'

The Rector sighed, and Mrs. Dengelton looked curiously at him, as if she guessed the meaning of the sigh, then resumed her story without commenting thereon, to Carriston's evident relief.

'Rudolph in some way came to hear of these stolen meetings, and surprised Austin walking with Rose one June evening. The brothers came—I regret to say—to blows, while Rose looked on in horror. Austin, being the younger and weaker, could not stand against the furious onslaught of Rudolph, who stunned him with a blow, then, thinking he had killed him, kissed Rose, who had fainted, and disappeared for ever. He returned to London, left the army, and went away to the East, with a considerable sum of money which he inherited from his mother.'

'And my father and mother?' asked Maurice breathlessly.

'Were found by some labourers insensible; the one from fear, the other from the blow given to him by his brother. They were taken to their respective homes, and when Austin got well again, he married Rose in due course. I believe your father and mother were very happy in their married life, Maurice, but they were singularly unfortunate in the fate of their children. Your brothers and sisters, four of them born during the early period of the marriage, all died; and you, who came into the world nearly twenty years after the marriage, were the only child who lived.'

'And how long ago did all this happen, aunt?'

'Cannot you think it out for yourself?' said Mrs. Dengelton tartly. 'You are now thirty-five; you were born—let me see—about fifteen years after the marriage, so altogether Rudolph disappeared fifty years ago.'

'And has not been heard of since?'

'No; all inquiries were made, but nothing came of them,' replied the lady, shaking her head. 'I suppose Rudolph thought he had killed Austin, and left England to avoid arrest. At all events, not a soul has heard of him since. Where he went, no one knows; but by this time, I have no doubt, he is dead.'

'Poor Uncle Rudolph, what an unhappy fate!' said Maurice thoughtfully.

'Ah, I always did blame Rose for that quarrel!' cried Mrs. Dengelton sourly.

'My mother'—began Maurice indignantly, when the Rector stopped him.

'Your mother was not to blame, my dear Maurice,' he said, rising to his feet. 'I know more about this story than Mrs. Dengelton thinks.'

A sniff was the Hon. Mrs. Dengelton's only reply, which was vulgar, but eloquent of disbelief.

Carriston's face, generally ruddy, was now somewhat pale, and Maurice wondered what could be the reason for such a loss of colour. The old man saw his inquiring look, and arose to take his leave.

'I must say good-night, my dear Maurice,' he said, giving his hand to Mrs. Dengelton. 'I am not so young as I once was, and keep early hours.'

At this moment, as if guided by some happy fate, Eunice, in company with Crispin, entered the room at the back of Mrs. Dengelton, and returned to their seats without her having noticed their absence.

'Good-night, sir,' said Crispin, coming forward to shake hands with the Rector.

'How quiet you have been!' remarked Mrs. Dengelton suspiciously. 'Where is my daughter?'

'Here, mamma;' and Eunice came forward in the demurest manner.

'Were you listening to my story?' asked her mother inquiringly,—'my story about your Uncle Rudolph leaving England?'

'No,' interposed Crispin quickly, before Eunice could speak; 'we were discussing photographs on yonder sofa.'

'Photographs, eh?' said Mrs. Dengelton, with a

frown, for she knew what looking over a photograph album meant in this case, but did not see her way to make further remark.

The Rector said good-night to every one, and then departed, accompanied by Maurice, who walked with him as far as the park gates. After Maurice had promised faithfully to call at the Rectory the next day, they separated, and the old clergyman went home, while his pupil returned to the Grange deep in his own thoughts.

'I wonder,' he said to himself, pausing for a moment in the shadowy avenue,—'I wonder if my uncle is still alive. If he is, I am wrongfully in possession of Roylands. Suppose he were to come back and claim it, I should once more be penniless. Well,' he sighed, resuming his walk, 'perhaps that would be the best thing that could happen, for work means happiness, and earning one's bread forces a man to take a deep interest in life whether he will or no.'

CHAPTER III.

THE RECTOR'S ROMANCE.

In pity for our painful strife
God aids us from above,
And every mortal in his life
Once plucks the rose of love.

The flower may bloom, the flower may fade,
As love brings joys or woes,
Still in the heart of youth and maid
That sacred blossom grows.

'Tis cherished thro' declining years,
Amid death's coming glooms,
And watered by regretful tears,
The flower eternal blooms.

Nor death that rose from us can part,
For when the body dies,
All broken on the broken heart,
That bud of heaven lies.

OYLANDS RECTORY was a comfortable-
looking house, distant about a mile from
the Grange, and near the village, which
was an extremely small one. Indeed, although the

parish was of fair dimensions, the Rector's con-
gregation was not large, and his clerical occupation
entailed but little work. Nevertheless, Stephen
Carriston did his best to attend to the spiritual welfare of the souls under his charge ; and if the hardest
day's work still left him with plenty of spare time on
his hands, that could hardly be called his fault. The
Rector abhorred idleness, which is said to be the
mother of all the vices, and managed to fill up his
leisure hours in a sufficiently pleasant manner by
indulging in occupations congenial to his tastes. He
was now engaged in translating the comedies of
Aristophanes into English verse, and found the biting
wit of the great Athenian playwright very delightful
after the dull brains of his parishioners. For the rest,
he pottered about his garden and attended to his
roses, which were the pride of his heart, as well they
might be, seeing that his small plot of ground was a
perfect bower of loveliness.

It is at this point that the pen fails and the brush
should come in ; for it would be simply impossible
to give in bald prose an adequate description of the
paradise of flowers contained within the red brick
walls which enclosed the garden on three sides. The
fourth side was the house, a quaint, low-roofed, old-

fashioned place, with deep diamond-paned lattices, and stacks of curiously-twisted chimneys. Built in the reign of the Second Charles, it yet bore the date of its erection, 1666, the *annus mirabilis* of Dryden, when half London was swept away by the fire, and half its inhabitants by the plague. Rector Carriston liked this house,—nay, like is too weak a word, he loved it,—as its antiquity, matching with his own, pleased him ; and besides, having resided under its red-tiled roof for over thirty years, it was natural that he should be deeply attached to its quaint walls and still quainter rooms.

But the garden! oh, the garden was a miracle of beauty! and only Crispin, who deals in such loveli-nesses, could describe its perfections, as he did indeed long afterwards, when the good Rector was dead, and could not read the glowing verse which eulogised his roses. Three moderately high brick walls, one running parallel to the high road, so that the Rector could keep a vigilant eye on the incomings and outgoings of his villagers, fenced in this modern garden of Alcinous, and these three walls were almost hidden by the foliage of peach and apricot and nectarine, for it was now midsummer, and Nature was decked out in her gayest robes. A dial in the middle of the smooth lawn, with its warning motto, which the Rector did not believe, as Time only sauntered with him ; a noble elm, wherein the thrush fluted daily, and a bower of greenery, in which the nightingale piped nightly : it was truly an ideal retreat, rendered still more perfect by the roses. The roses ! oh, the red, white, and yellow roses ! how they bloomed in profusion under the old red wall, which drew the heat of the sun into its breast, and then showered it second-hand on the delicate, warmth-loving flowers. Great creamy buds, trembling amid their green leaves at the caress of the wind ; gorgeous crimson blossoms, burning incense to the hot sun ; pale-tinted flowers, which flushed delicately at the dawn hour ; and bright yellow orbs, which looked as though the touch of Midas had turned them into gold. All the bees for miles around knew that garden, and the finest honey in the neighbourhood owed its existence to the constant visits they paid to this wilderness of sweets.

Such a bright morning as it was ! Above, the blue sky, in which the sun burned lustily ; below, the green earth, pranked with flowers ; and between these two splendours, the Rector, armed with a pair of scissors,

strolling contentedly about his small domain.   From
the adjacent fields, where the corn was yet young,
sprang a brown-feathered lark, which rose higher
and higher in spiral circles, singing as though his
throat would burst with melody, until, the highest
point attained, he ceased his liquid warblings and
fell earthward like a stone.   Indeed, the Rector had
no lack of music, for the larks awoke him in the
morning, the thrushes piped to him at noon, and
when night fell the divine nightingale pouring forth
her impassioned strains wooed him from his study,
where he was reading the Aristophanic rendering of
her song, to listen to the reality, before which even
the magical Greek verse seemed harsh.   'Twas an
ideal place, and in it the Rector lived an ideal
existence, far away from the noise and restlessness
of our modern civilisation.   In his study he had the
books of genius, which he greatly loved, but in his
garden he possessed the book of God, which he loved
still more ; and even had not he been a devout
believer in the goodness of the Almighty, surely
that garden would have converted him with its dewy
splendours.

An odd figure looked Mr. Carriston, shuffling
about in a pair of comfortable old slippers, a very

raven in blackness, save for the wide-brimmed straw hat shading his grey hairs, his benevolent-looking face. With a green watering-pan in one hand, and the scissors in the other, he pryed and peered among his beloved flowers, with his two pets—a cat and a magpie—at his heels, and clipped off a dead leaf here, plucked a withered blossom there, with the tenderest anxiety for the well-being of the roses.

'Dear, dear!' sighed the Rector, pausing before a drooping-looking Gloire de Dijon; 'this does not seem at all healthy. It needs rain—in fact, I think the flowers would be none the worse for a shower or so; but there's no sign of rain,' looking anxiously up to the cloudless sky. 'I wonder if a little manure'—

Down went the Rector on his knees, and began grubbing about the roots of the plant, much to the discomfort of the magpie, who hopped about near him in an agitated manner.

'A brass thimble,' said Mr. Carriston, making a discovery, 'a copper, and three blue beads. The roots of the plant wounded, too, with scratching. This is your work, Simon. I wish you would hide your rubbish somewhere else.'

The magpie, otherwise Simon, made a vicious peck at the Rector's hand, to revenge himself for the discovery of his treasure; then, anxious to save something, snatched up the thimble and made off hastily.

'Too bad of Simon,' murmured Mr. Carriston, rubbing his nose in a vexed manner. 'I shall have to ask Mukle to keep him in the back yard. Ah, Mukle! what is it?'

Mukle—to the Rector, Mrs. Mukle to her friends —was a hard-featured, bony woman, who looked as if she had been cut out of a deal board. Her cooking was much more agreeable than her appearance, and, having been with the Rector—whom she adored—for many years, she knew to a turn what he liked and what he did not like, therefore suited him admirably, in her double capacity of cook and housekeeper.

'Mr. Roylands, sir!' announced Mukle grimly.

'Oh, where is he?'

'Study, sir,' responded Mukle, who was a lady with a firm belief in the golden rule of silence.

'Ask him to come here.'

An assenting sniff was Mukle's only reply, and, turning on her heel in a military fashion,—the late Mr. Mukle had been a soldier,—she strode back to the house like a grenadier.

Meanwhile, Mr. Carriston, having risen to his feet,

was dusting his knees, and, while thus engaged, saw Maurice coming towards him. Assuredly the master of the Grange was a fine specimen of humanity, for he was over six feet in height, and, being arrayed in shooting-coat, knickerbockers, and deerstalker's hat, looked remarkably striking. He would have looked better had his face borne a smile, but, as it was, he came solemnly forward and took the Rector's outstretched hand, as if he was chief mourner at a funeral.

'You shouldn't be a country gentleman, Maurice,' said Mr. Carriston, after the usual greetings had been exchanged. 'The occupation of a monk would suit you better.'

Maurice said nothing, but sighed wearily.

'Come now, my dear lad; if you sigh in that fashion, I shall suspect you of being a lover, in spite of your asseveration to the contrary.'

'A man can't marry his aunt, and as Crispin wants to marry Eunice, there is no one left for me but my honourable relation.'

'Try Mukle.'

'Too much of a grenadier.'

'I think you are the same—in height,' said the Rector, looking approvingly at his tall friend. 'If

old Father Fritz had seen the pair of ye, I think
he would have insisted upon the marriage, so as
to breed a race of giants. But, dear, dear! what
nonsense we talk! Come and sit down, my lad.
Will you smoke?'

'No, thank you, sir. I'm tired of smoking.'

'Maurice, if you go on in this fashion, I shall be
angry with you. It's a beautiful day, so you ought
to have a beautiful smile on your face. Listen to
that lark! Does not its gush of song thrill your
heart? Admire my roses! Where, even in the
gorgeous East, will you see such splendour? The
birds sing, the sun shines, the flowers bloom, and
yet you are as discontented as if you were shut up
between four bare walls. Maurice, I'm really and
truly ashamed of your ingratitude to God for His
many gifts.' Maurice made no reply, but punched
holes in the gravel with his walking-stick. 'Now
you wait here, my lad,' said the Rector, recovering
breath after his little lecture, 'and see if yon lark
can sing you into a better frame of mind. It may
be the David to your Saul, and drive the evil spirit
out of you. I am going away to wash my hands,
which are somewhat grubby with my gardening, and
will return in a few moments.'

Off went the Rector with an elastic step, as springy as that of a young man, and Maurice looked after him in sheer envy of such light-heartedness.

'Why cannot I be happy like that?' he sighed, baring his head to the cool breeze.

Did ever a man ask himself so ridiculous a question! Here was a healthy young man, of good personal appearance, with a superfluity of the gifts of fortune, yet he commiserated himself for nothing at all, and propounded riddles to himself which he was unable to answer. But all such misery came from incessant brooding and self-analysis, which is bound in the long-run to make even the most complacent person dissatisfied with his advantages. If Maurice, throwing aside his books, art, broodings, and everything else, had gone in for fishing, hunting, dancing, rowing, as he did in his earlier youth, his mind would soon have resumed its normal healthiness. Unluckily, the ten years' life in Bohemia, where he had neither money nor time to indulge in such sports, had weakened his interest in them, and he by no means seemed inclined to take up the broken thread of his life. This was a great mistake, as, had he reverted to his earlier mode of living, he would in a short time have come to look upon that weary decade as but a bad dream, and ultimately have recovered the *mens sana in corpore sano* condition, which is so essential to the happiness of one's existence. If there is a person to be envied, 'tis a healthy man with an average stock of brains, for he does not live with shadows, he has no torturing dreams, he does not rack his soul with thinking out the problems of life ; but simply takes the goods the gods provide, enjoys them to the full measure of his capacity, and throws all disturbing influences to the winds. Maurice Roylands was a man of this sort in many respects, but he had a trifle too much brain power, and therefore, in accordance with the great law of compensation, suffered from the excess, by using it to torture his otherwise healthy mind. Unfortunately, he did not reason in this way, but, feeling that he was miserable, hastily decided that such misery was incurable. Not a wise way of looking at the matter certainly, but then Maurice, though no fool in many ways, was not a Solomon for wisdom ; and besides, Melancholia, who places all things in a dull light, had him in her grip, and prevented him from giving his diseased mind the medicine it required.

However, in accordance with his old tutor's in-

structions, he sat there in silence, drinking in the
odours of the flowers, and listening to the music of
the lark. Not only that, but a thrush in the tree
above him began to pour forth his mellow notes;
and, though it was nigh mid-June, he heard the
quaint call of the cuckoo sound in the distance.
Nature and Nature's voices exercised their benign
influence on his restless spirit, and even in that
short space of time soothed him so much that, when
Mr. Carriston returned, he missed the frowning face
with which Maurice had greeted him.

'Ah,' said the Rector, with a nod of satisfaction, 'you have benefited by the music of the birds
already. I would undertake to cure you, if you
would only let me be your physician. Now your
soul is more at rest, but I have no doubt your nerves
need soothing, so try this churchwarden and this
excellent tobacco.'

Maurice burst out laughing at this odd cure for
melancholy, but did not refuse the Rector's hospitality; and any one who entered the garden a few
minutes afterwards, would have discovered the vener-
able Rector and the youthful Squire puffing gravely
at long clays, like two cronies in a village taproom.

They chatted in a desultory manner of little things,

such as Mrs. Dengelton,—who would have been very
angry to find herself placed in such a category,—
Eunice, love-making, Crispin, the home farm, and
such-like trifles, when, after a short pause, Maurice
abruptly turned to the Rector, who, lying back in
luxurious ease, was watching the trembling of the
leaves above his head.

'And the story, Rector?'

This question brought Mr. Carriston from heaven
to earth, and he looked at the young man with a
grave smile on his face.

'Ah, the story,' he repeated, laying aside his pipe.
'Yes, I promised to tell you the one romance of my
life. I am afraid it is a very prosaic romance, still it
may show you how a man can find life endurable
even after his heart is broken.'

'Why, Rector, is your heart broken?'

'I thought it was once, but I'm afraid 'twas mended
long ago. *Et ego in Arcadia fui*, Maurice, although
you would never think so to look at me. Tush! what
has an old man pottering about among his flowers in
common with Cupid, god of love? Yet I, too, have
sported with Amaryllis in the shade, and piped love-
songs to the careless ear of Neæra.'

He sighed a trifle sadly, very probably somewhat

regretful of that dead and gone romance which still
looked bright through the mists of forty years, and
glanced sorrowfully at the wrinkled hands which had
once played with the golden tresses of Chloe. Ah,
Chloe was old now, and her famous golden locks were
white with the snows of many winters; or perchance
she was dead, with the gentle winds blowing across her
daisied grave, and piping songs as beautiful as those
of her faithful shepherd. Is it not a painful thing to
be old and grey and full of sad memories of our fine
days? yet, mingled with such melancholics, we recall
many bright dreams which then haunted our youthful brains. Alas, Arcady! why are we not permitted
to dwell for ever in thy flowery meadows, beneath
thy blue sky, instead of being driven forth by the
whip of Fate to crowded cities and desolate wastes,
wherein sound no gleeful melodies.

'It was at Oxford that I first met her,' said the
Rector in his mellow voice, which was touched with
vague regret; 'for she, too, dwelt in that grave schol-
astic city. I was not in holy orders then! No; my
ambition was to be a soldier, and win the V.C.; but,
alas! such dreams came to nought. You may not
believe it, Maurice, but I was wild and light-hearted
in those days—to be sure, it was Consule Planco, and

youth is ever foolish. Her name was Miriam, and
she was a dressmaker. Ah, you are astonished that
I, Stephen Carriston, fixed my eyes on such a lowly
damsel; but then, you see, I loved her dearly, and
that, I think, is a sufficient answer to your unspoken
objection. Love knows nothing of rank or position,
and sees beauty in the wayside daisy as well as in
the costly hothouse plant. I need not tell you she
was very beautiful, for that is the common saying of
lovers, who behold no loveliness save in the nymph
of their affections. What is it the poet says about a
lover seeing Helen's beauty in the brow of Egypt?
Sure, my memory is weak with age, and I mis-
quote. Still, the saying is true. Miriam was very
beautiful, and I think must have had some Jewish
blood in her veins, for her dark, imperial beauty was
that of the East. Her hair was as dark as the wing
of a raven, her eyes liquid wells of light, and her
mouth was as the thread of scarlet spoken of in
the song of the wise king. You see, Maurice, old as
I am, I can still rhapsodise on Chloe's perfections,
though she basely deceived me. Alas, Strephon!
how the years have destroyed thy goddess!—nay,
she destroyed herself by her own act.'

'I did not know you were a poet, Rector.'

Mr. Carriston, whose brow was dark with bitter memories, aroused himself with a forced laugh, and strove to speak lightly of the past.

'Live and learn, Maurice. I no poet? Why, my dear lad, I am even now courting the Nine, and turning Aristophanes into good English verse. No poet? Why, every man is a poet when in love; and if he does not write a poem, he at least lives a poem. I, alas, have been in love these many years with a shadow—the shadow of Miriam before she left me!'

'Left you?'

'Yes. I call it my romance, but it is a painful story. A deceitful woman, a wronged man, a treacherous friend—a common enough tale, I think. Though, indeed, I need not include "friend," for to this day I know not for whom she left me.'

'She was your wife?'

'Yes. Wild as I was in those days, I was too honourable to deceive a woman. In spite of the difference of our position, I married her, and we were happy together for ten years.'

'Ten years!' replied Maurice in surprise. 'Surely she did not leave you after all that time of married happiness.'

'Who knows the ways of women?' said the Rector

bitterly. ' Yes, she left me—took from me all I loved in the world, herself and her child.'

' Was there a child?'

' Yes. He was born in the tenth year of our marriage, just when I had given up all hope of being a father. If he be still alive, Maurice, he will just be five years younger than you,—thirty years old,—and for that I love you, my dear lad; you stand to me in the place of the son I have lost.'

' Did you not suspect any one of taking her away?'

' Yes; one man,' answered the Rector gloomily. ' He was a tall, black-bearded fellow, who had just come back from the East; but I only saw him once. I was a hard-worked London curate in those days, and had but little time to spare. My wife met him —I think his name was Captain Malcolm—at the house of a mutual friend ; but perhaps I am wrong, and it was not he who destroyed my happiness. She had so many friends. I can hardly wonder at that, for she was then in the full pride of her womanly beauty. There was a Frenchman, the Count de la Tour, whom I also suspected, but I was sure of no one. I suppose she grew tired of our poor life ; for, in spite of the way in which she went into society, we were poor —that is, comfortable for a quiet life, but too poor for a social one. I, never suspecting any evil, was only too glad that she should go out and enjoy herself, although at times I remonstrated with her, saying that such gaiety was not suited for the wife of a poor clergyman. She said she would give up such frivolities shortly, and I, like a fool, believed her. Then I was called down to see my father, who was very ill. At length he died, and I remained to attend to the funeral; but on returning to London after a three weeks' absence, I found she was gone and the child also. She left no letter behind her to palliate her guilt; all I knew was that she had departed with some gentleman who had called for her in a brougham. The servants could not describe the man, as he did not enter the house, but remained in the carriage. My false wife told the servants she was summoned by me, as her father-in-law was dying ; and it was only when I returned that they learned the truth.'

'Did you ever see this Captain Malcolm again ?'

'No, nor the Count de la Tour ; so that is why I suspect one of those men as being the ruin of my life. Besides, I heard afterwards that she went a great deal about with them, sometimes with one, sometimes with the other. One of them I am sure it was, but I know

not which. So you see, at one blow, Maurice, I was
bereft of wife, child, home, and happiness. Afterwards I was offered this living, and, wishing to leave
the scene of my former happiness, my former sorrow,
my former disgrace, I accepted it, and came down
here, where I have lived in peace for thirty years.'

'Did you get a divorce?'

'Yes; for the sake of my guilty wife. I did not
wish to marry again myself, but I desired to leave her
free, so that she might wed the partner of her guilt.
I hope he behaved honourably, and made her his
wife; but, alas! I know not.'

'And the boy?'

'I have never heard of him since. I was left rich
by the death of my father, and all that money could
do was done, but I heard nothing of either wife or
child. Is it not a sad story, Maurice?'

'Yes, very sad! You must have suffered terribly.'

'I did suffer terribly; but I tell you this, dear lad,
to show you how a man can force himself to be cheerful, even when he thinks life has no further joys for
him. Look at me! When my wife left me, I thought
that the sun of my life had set for ever. I looked
forward to years of misery; and probably my existence would have been miserable, had I not, with

the aid of God, resisted the evil one. I did resist him, by accustoming myself to take an interest in all things ; and, by schooling myself into patience, I found life, if not blissful, at least endurable. I now love my work among my parishioners, I enjoy my Greek studies, I interest myself in my garden, and am thus able to live a comparatively happy life. Had I given way to my misery, I would have been an unhappy man all my life, and have done no good in my generation ; but I fought against the evil spirit, with the aid of God I conquered him, and now can look back with thankfulness to the calamity which tried and chastened my soul.'

'And you are happy now ? '

'Yes,' said the Rector firmly. 'I am as happy as any mortal can hope to be. "Man is born to trouble as the sparks fly upward," says Job ; but if we did not fight against these troubles they would overwhelm us. So, my dear lad, do as I have done, fight against the evil spirit, and, with God's grace, you will be victorious.'

'I thank you for your advice, sir, and I will try and follow it.'

'My story is but a dull one, I am afraid,' resumed the Rector, after a pause,—'dull and prosaic, with no

romance to render it captivating ; but I only told it
to you to show you what a man can do if he fights
against his troubles, and does not yield weakly to the
first attack of the enemy. You have no unhappy
love, you have no regrets ; therefore, my dear lad,
show yourself to be a man, and do not thus tamely
surrender to a phantom of your own creation. Try
to be interested in life, fall in love and marry if you
can, and I promise you all will yet be well with you.
Your troubles are but dreams of a disordered brain,
which can be banished by an effort of will ; so rouse
yourself, Maurice, conquer your weak spirit, and with
God's help you will be a happy man.'

'Thank you, sir,' said Maurice, grasping the Rector's
hand ; 'I will do what you say. I have been weak,
but I will be so no longer. I will take up the duties
of life, and do my best to perform them well. Your
sermon, your story, has done me good, Mr. Carriston ;
and I feel that I should indeed be a coward to flinch
from the fray in which you have so bravely fought and
conquered.'

'Good lad! good lad!' replied the delighted Rector.
'I knew you would see things in their right light.
But come, the lesson is over, and now is the time for
play. You must look round at my roses, and the

finest bud of the garden shall adorn your buttonhole as "a reward for your determination." '

Maurice gladly fell in with the Rector's humour, and together they strolled round the garden to examine and admire his floral treasures. Carriston was like a child in his garden, and his bursts of delight at this or that particular rose tree would have made many a person smile. But Maurice did not smile ; he loved his old tutor too well to ridicule his simple pleasures, and took scarcely less interest than the Rector himself in the momentous question of transferring this tree over there, or of grafting a hardy shoot on to this sickly-looking plant here. Suddenly the Rector stopped, and began to rummage in the pockets of his long black coat.

'Dear, dear!' he said in a vexed tone ; 'it is not here, and yet I am sure I placed it in this pocket.'

'Placed what, sir ? '

'A letter ! a letter ! No, I can't find it. Maurice, I wish you to stay to luncheon. I have a friend coming.'

'Indeed ? '

'Well, not exactly a friend; but, the fact is, a young man has arrived in the village with a letter of introduction to me from a mutual friend in London.

He is at present staying at the Royland Arms, and sent in his letter this morning, so I wrote back and asked him to come to luncheon. You must stay and meet him, Maurice, for I hear he is a most delightful man.'

'What is his name?'

'I cannot remember. He is a Greek. The letter must be in my study, so we will go and look for it. This young Greek is a great traveller, and is now on a visit to England. He had a letter of introduction to my friend, the Archdeacon of Eastminster, who gave him one to me.'

'But what does he come to this out-of-the-way place for?' asked Maurice, with that inherent suspicion he had acquired in Bohemia.

'I don't know. I expect he will answer that question for himself at luncheon. Ah, here is the letter—I left it on the table.'

'Well, what is his name?' asked Maurice again.

The Rector adjusted his *pince-nez*, and, smoothing open the letter, read the name aloud :—

'Count Constantine Caliphronas.'

CHAPTER IV.

A MASTERPIECE OF NATURE.

The pride of the human
  Does Nature diminish,
With spiteful acumen,
  She roughly will finish
A man or a woman,
  He stout and she thinnish,
Till one is not fair, nor the other a true man.

But Nature's conception
  May not be pernicious,
For know her perception
  At times is capricious:
Her work bears inspection,
  In manner judicious,
For sometimes she turns out a man near perfection.

THE above jingle of verses may sound somewhat abstruse, but he who has the patience
to search until he discovers the kernel of
this rhyming nut, will certainly find it to be a truism.
Nature does finish the mass of humanity in a somewhat rough and ready fashion; true, she may equip

them with all the limbs and organs necessary
to the enjoyment of life, but she does not trouble
herself to put in those delicate touches which go
to the making of a perfectly handsome man, or a
faultlessly beautiful woman.　At times, however,
just to show what she can do in the way of creative
beauty, she gives her whole mind to the task, and
lo! Achilles and Helen of Troy.　But such perfect
specimens of humanity are few and far between;
therefore when Maurice, who had an artistic eye, met
Count Constantine Caliphronas for the first time, he
recognised with delight that he saw before him one
of Nature's masterpieces.

There is nothing more detestable than that society
horror, 'a beauty man,' who resembles a wax figure
in his unnatural perfectability of face and form.
Flawless he may be in every part, but the ensemble
is nevertheless displeasing both to eye and mind, for,
in aiding Nature to show herself at her best, he soon
becomes a mere artificial figure, which ought to be
placed in a glass case for the edification of school
misses and gushing society ladies.　This man,
however, did not belong to that over-civilised class,
as at a glance one could see he was a child of Nature,
a nursling of the winds and waves, whose physical

perfections were kept in their pristine beauty by the constant care of the great mother herself. Caliphronas had all the grace and untamed beauty of a wild animal, and looked as if he claimed kinship with the salt sea, the fresh woods, the strong sunlight, and the bracing air of snow-clad mountain-tops. His physical beauty was truly wonderful, and was as much the outcome of perfect health, as of perfect creation. He lacked that self-restrained air which is stamped on the face of every civilised man, and in the modest little dining-room of the Rectory he was like some graceful panther caged against its will. Nature's child was only in his right place with Nature herself, and in our dull respectable England he seemed an exile from the healthful solitudes which had given him birth.

'It is impossible to describe Caliphronas,' said Maurice many years afterwards, in speaking of this man. 'I can tell you that his figure was as perfect as that of the Apollo Belvedere, and say that his face was as flawless in its virile beauty as is the Antinous of the Vatican, but this will give you small idea of his physical perfection. His body seemed to be instinct with the lawless fierceness of wind and wave; he moved with the stately grace of a nude savage unaccustomed to the restraint of clothing. I never understood the phrase "child of Nature" until I saw Caliphronas, and it is the only way in which he can be explained. I believe his mother was a Nereid and his father a hunter, for he was the offspring of earth and ocean—the consummate flower of both. Yet I do not think he had what we call brains—true, he possessed the cunning and instinct of a wild animal, but that was all. I think, myself, brains and culture would have spoiled him ; he was born to be a wild, free thing, happy only on the hills, a type, a visible incarnation of Nature in a male form. If you ask me whom he resembled in real life, I cannot tell you, as I never saw any one in the least like him. But in fiction—well, study the character of Margrave in *A Strange Story*, and Donatello in Hawthorne's *Marble Faun*, and by blending the two you may arrive at some conception of Count Caliphronas.'

Such was the man who now sat at the table of the Rector, chatting gaily with his host and Maurice Roylands. Being a hot day, the Rector had wisely provided a cold luncheon, and himself presided over a noble piece of beef, which looked as though it had been taken from one of Apollo's oxen. There was also a capital salad,—the Rector was famous for his salads,—fruit, wine, cheese, and bread. A simple repast, truly, but then the Rector was simple in his tastes, and detested those highly-spiced dishes, which but create thirst, and whose chief merit seems to be that the diner cannot tell of what they are composed. An artificial life creates artificial tastes, and the principal mission of cookery now seems to lie in the direction of tickling the palate, not of satisfying the appetite, with the result that gout and dyspepsia have it all their own way. If half, nay, if the whole of the French cooks now engaged in ruining the healths of Englishmen and Englishwomen were bundled back to their beloved Paris, the income of every doctor in London would decrease with the rapidity of lightning. As before mentioned, the Rector liked the good things of this life, but he thought the simplest food the most enjoyable, in which he was right, though epicures may doubt the truth of such an opinion. Yet, after all, do not epicures hold the simplicity of a well-roasted leg of mutton to be a dish fit for a king ? For information on this point read Brillat Savarin.

If the Rector was simple in his eating, however, Count Constantine was still more so, for he hardly touched his meat, and confined his attention to bread, cheese, salad, and wine—the latter being excellent claret, on which the Rector prided himself.

'My dear sir,' he said in agony, as he saw Caliphronas about to mingle water with his wine, 'you will spoil the flavour of the claret.'

'Pardon me, sir,' replied the Count, who spoke English admirably, 'but we Greeks are partial to such mingling. We worship the Naiad with her urn as well as Bacchus with his flask, and the union of both produces a drink fit for Father Zeus.'

'You don't seem to care much for meat,' said the Rector, relinquishing the point about the wine, though it went to his soul to see such a spoiling of the finest qualities of his claret.

'No,' answered Caliphronas carelessly; 'oddly enough, I do not care much for flesh. I dwell so much in the open air that, like Nature, I live on the simplest things. Bread, cheese, and wine I love; add honey, and I want nothing better to satisfy my appetite. Country fare for a country man, you know.'

'You are a shepherd of Theocritus,' said Maurice, with a smile.

'No; save in such tastes perhaps; otherwise I am no Sicilian of the Idylles.'

'You speak English wonderfully well, Count,' remarked the Rector politely.

'Thank you for the compliment, sir ; yet this is the first time I have been in England.'

'What! do they teach English in the schools of Athens?'

'Alas, no. The schools of modern Athens are not those of the old Greek days. Socrates, Plato, Pythagoras, have gone to the blessed isles in company with the heroes of Salamis, and our Greek culture of to-day is primitive in the extreme. No; I learned English from a roving Englishman—a scholar and a gentleman who grew weary of this respectable England of yours, and came back to the freer life of the Greek islands.'

'He taught you admirably,' said Roylands, wondering why the Greek eyed him so keenly while making this speech. 'Do you come from Athens?'

'I have been there,' answered Caliphronas, pushing away his plate, 'but I am an islander. Yes, I was born in Ithaca, therefore am I a countryman of Ulysses.'

'Achilles, perhaps,' observed the Rector, fascinated by the clear-cut features of the young man,—'the godlike Achilles.'

'Ah no,' replied the Greek, with a shade of melancholy in his tone; 'I am like no hero of those times. Our ancestors have transmitted to us their physical forms, but not their brains, not their heroism.'

'Come now,' remonstrated Maurice. 'I am sure your countrymen behaved bravely in the War of Independence.'

'Yes, I agree with you there. Canaris, Mavrocordato, Bozartis, were all brave men. I accept the rebuke, for I have no right to run down my own countrymen. Perhaps in England I may learn the meaning of the word patriotism.'

'Or Jingoism.'

'Your pardon?' queried the Count, a trifle puzzled.

'Jingoism,' explained Maurice gravely, 'is a spurious patriotism, composed of music-hall songs, the Union Jack, and gallons of beer—it begins with a chorus and ends with a riot. Tom, Dick, and Harry are very fond of it, as it expands their lungs and quenches their thirst. But there, I am only jesting. Do you stay long in England?'

Again the Greek eyed Maurice keenly, and hesitated a moment before replying.

'I can hardly tell yet,' he said, with emphasis.

'Mr. Carriston, will you show me your garden?' he added, turning to the Rector.

'I shall be delighted,' said Carriston eagerly; 'we will stroll round it. Do you smoke?'

'No, thank you,' returned the Count, waving away with a gesture of repugnance the cigarette Maurice held out to him. 'I never smoke.'

'That is strange.'

Caliphronas shrugged his shoulders.

'Perhaps so, sir. For myself, I do not care about it.'

'Curious creature,' murmured Maurice reflectively, as he followed the Rector and his guest into the garden. 'I wonder why he looks at me so keenly, and what he is doing down here. Humph! I would like to find out your little game, my friend.'

Ten years of fighting with the world had turned Maurice from a frank, open-hearted fellow into a cold, suspicious man, and he always doubted the motives of every one. This is a disagreeable way of looking at things, but in many cases it is a very necessary one, owing to the double lives which most people seem now-a-days to live. Social intercourse, whether for pleasure or business, is no longer as simple as it used to be in the old days, and our complex civilisation has introduced into every action we perform that element of distrust which is at once disagreeable and necessary. Maurice knew nothing about Caliphronas, and had he met him in London would doubtless have accepted him for what he appeared to be—a foreign nobleman on his travels ; but for this man to visit a quiet village like Roylands was peculiar, and there must be some motive for his so doing.

'I'll ask him how he likes England, and lead up to his unexpected arrival here,' thought Maurice, as he walked along smoking his cigarette. 'He seems sharp, but I think I'm able to distinguish between the real and the false.'

Caliphronas was loud in his expressions of admiration for the Rector's roses, and his delight seemed genuine enough even to Maurice, who stood listening to his raptures with a grim smile, as if he would like to cast over this bright being the shadow of his own melancholy nature.

'I have a perfect passion for flowers,' said the Count, with a gay smile, as he placed a red bud in his coat, 'and roses are my favourites. Were they not the flowers of pleasure in classical times? did they not wreathe the brows of revellers at festivals?—the flowers of love and of silence !'

' I am pleased you like flowers,' observed the Rector, looking at the joyous figure before him, which was bathed in sunshine ; ''tis an innocent pleasure.'

' I love all that is of Nature,' cried Caliphronas, throwing himself on the smooth sward ; ' Nature is my mother—my true mother. Yes, I am a man born of woman, but such maternity does not appeal to me. Nature is at once my mother, my nurse, my goddess.'

' You were born in Ithaca,' asked Maurice inquiringly.

' Was I born at all ? ' replied Caliphronas, throwing himself back with a joyous laugh and letting the sun blaze on his uncovered head. ' I do not know ! I cannot tell. Perchance some nymph bore me to one of the old gods, who Heine says yet walk the earth in other forms.'

' What do you know of Heine ? ' asked the Rector in some surprise.

' Nothing !—absolutely nothing. I never heard his name till the other day, when some one told me a story of the Gods in Exile, and said one Heine had written it.'

' Are you fond of reading ? '

' I never read. I care not for books—all my knowledge comes from the mouth of my fellow-men and from Nature. Such culture is enough for me.'

'You will get a sunstroke if you don't cover your head,' said Maurice, somewhat tired of this pseudo-classicism.

'No! I am a friend of Apollo's. He will hurl no darts at me, and your pale sun in England is but a shadow of the glorious Helios of our Greek skies.'

And, lying on his back, he began to sing a strange, wandering melody, of which the words (roughly trans-lated) were as follows :—

> *The sun is my father :*
> *He kissed my mother the sea,*
> *And of their wooing the fruit am I.*

Both Englishmen were singularly fascinated by this stranger. He conducted himself in quite an unconventional fashion, and seemed to follow the last thought that suggested itself to his capricious brain.

'Come!' he cried, springing to his feet with a bound like a deer. 'Come, Mr. Maurice—are you a runner? I will race you round this garden.'

'Really, Count,' said the Rector, somewhat startled.

'Eh! Am I wrong, sir?' replied Caliphronas apologetically. 'I ask your pardon! I do not know your English ways; you must teach me. I act as I feel. Is it wrong to do so?'

'Well, we English like to see a little more self-restraint,' said Maurice, looking at the graceful figure of the young man. 'By the way, are you going to stay here long?'

The smile faded from the bright face of the Count, and he turned half away with an abrupt movement.

'Who can tell?' he said lightly. 'I am a bird of passage. I alight here and there, but fly when I am weary of the bough. You wonder at my coming down here, do you not, Mr. Maurice?'

Thus addressed directly, Roylands was rather taken aback, and reddened perceptibly through the tan of his skin.

'Well, for a gay young man like you, Count, I thought London would have been more congenial.'

Caliphronas burst out laughing, and, putting his hands behind his head, leant back against the trunk of the elm:

'Do you hear your friend, sir?' he said to the Rector. 'He thinks that I prefer that dull, smoky town to the country. Why, Athens is too narrow for me! I love the open lands, the plains, the mountains,

the seas. Up in that city of yours I was weary, and
I spoke to the friend of my friend. "Oh," I cried, " I
will die of want of air in this place. Take me to the
woods, where I can breathe and see the sun." So he
gave me that letter to you,' addressing the Rector, 'and
I came here at once.'

So this was the explanation of his presence in the
little village—a very natural one surely, and Maurice
felt somewhat ashamed of his late suspicions; but a
new thought had entered his head, suggested by the
statuesque pose of the Greek leaning against the tree,
and he came forward eagerly.

'Count Caliphronas,' he said quickly, 'I am a
sculptor, and I have the idea for a statue of Endymion
—would you—would you '—

'Ah, you want me to be a model, sir?' said the
Count, laughing. 'Eh, well, I do not mind in the
least—you may command me.'

'Thank you very much, if I '—

'If you could only introduce me to a Diana, that
would indeed be perfect.'

'I suppose you are a kind of general lover, Count,'
said the Rector, turning round from a rose tree with a
smile.

'I am not as bad as that, sir. No! I love! I love!'

He stopped abruptly, and a shade came over his face. 'Yes, I love,' he resumed quickly; 'but my love is unfortunate.'

'What! is any woman cold-hearted enough to refuse you?' observed Maurice, looking at him in amazement; for indeed a woman would be hard to please were she not satisfied with this splendid-looking youth.

'There are women and women,' said Caliphronas enigmatically. 'This one does not love me yet, but she will.'

'When?'

The Greek shot a keen glance at Maurice, and then observed, in an indifferent voice,—

'When I do what I am requested to do.'

Both men looked steadily at one another, and it seemed to Maurice as though there were a certain amount of menace visible on the face of Caliphronas, but such look speedily passed away, and he bounded lightly across the turf to where the cat was sitting.

To the surprise of both the Rector and Maurice, she let this stranger take her up in his arms and smooth her fur.

'Dear, dear!' said the Rector in an astonished tone; 'what power do you possess over the animal world, Count? That cat will not let any one touch her as a rule.'

'Oh, all animals take to me,' replied Caliphronas lightly, letting the cat down gently on the ground. 'I can do anything with horses and dogs.'

'Donatello!' whispered Maurice to himself. 'He looks innocent enough, and yet that look—I must speak to Crispin, and ask his opinion of this man.'

Meanwhile the Count was giving Carriston a description of his miseries at the Royland Arms.

'Such a small room to sleep in,' he said in a disgusted tone. 'I know I shall be smothered if I stay in it. No; I shall wrap myself up in a blanket and sleep under the moon like Endymion, which will be training for your friend's statue.'

'That will be dangerous,' objected the Rector.

'Not at all! In Greece—I mean my native islands —I sleep out very often. Oh, there is nothing more beautiful than slumber in the open air. I cannot bear houses; they stifle me; they crush me. I love no roof lower than the sky. And then to wake at dawn, to see the east glow with rosy tints, to watch the dew moisten every blade of grass, the awakening of the animals, the first songs of the birds, and the

rising of the sun.   Oh, I worship the sun !   I worship
him !'

The Rector was a trifle shocked at this peroration,
as he was not quite sure whether this fantastic being
was not a sun-worshipper in downright earnest ;
the more so as in a sudden freak he flung himself
down on his knees and held out his arms to the
glorious luminary.

'You are joking,' he said gravely.

'Not I,' replied Caliphronas, springing to his feet.
'You are not angry, are you, sir? Eh! I forgot
myself you were a priest in this country. I must
explain. I am of the Greek Church—yes! oh, I
have been baptized.'

The Rector smiled, and said no more, for it was
impossible to talk seriously with a man who possessed
so childish a soul.   Meanwhile, Maurice, who had
been thinking over matters, came to the conclusion
that he would ask Caliphronas to stay at the Grange
for a few days.   At first sight this seemed rather in-
judicious, but when he remembered the high character
of the man who vouched for the respectability of the
Greek, all his scruples vanished.   Besides, Caliphronas
was such a peculiar character that he desired a closer
acquaintance with him ; and, above all, he could not

hope anywhere to find such a perfect model for his Endymion. Taking, then, all these facts into consideration, he speedily made up his mind to ask the Count to be his guest, and did so without delay.

'Count,' he said politely, 'I am afraid you will find that inn very uncomfortable, so I should be glad to see you at the Grange for a week or so, where I think you will find yourself in more civilised quarters.'

The Count's eyes flashed with what looked uncommonly like triumph, but he dropped the lids over them rapidly for the moment, so as to prevent this look being seen, and shook Maurice heartily by the hand.

'Thank you very much! oh, very much indeed!' he said effusively. 'I hope I will not trouble you. I will be glad to come—yes, that place in the village would kill me.'

'That's all right,' replied Maurice, who had an Englishman's horror of a scene. 'I will send over for your traps, and you can come to the Grange in time for dinner. We dine at seven o'clock.'

'Thank you, sir. I will be at your home to-night.'

The Rector, who had fully intended to ask Caliphronas to be his guest, was rather startled by Maurice's precipitancy, but, on the whole, was not ill-pleased, for two reasons : the first being that he did not much care about burdening himself with this eccentric foreigner ; and the second, that he was delighted that, during the stay of the Count at the Grange, Maurice would take to his modelling again.

'By the way,' said Maurice, turning suddenly to the Count, 'do you know any one called Crispin ?'

'Crispin !' repeated Caliphronas, with his foreign accent ; 'no, I do not know that name.'

'He is a gentleman who is staying with me,' replied Roylands carelessly ; 'and, as he is pretty well acquainted with your part of the world, I thought you might have met him.'

Caliphronas smilingly denied that he had the honour of Crispin's acquaintance, but it seemed to Maurice as though there was a shade of apprehension on the Greek's face, and he felt somewhat puzzled thereat.

'Can't make this fellow out,' was his mental comment. 'Hope I'm not making a mistake in asking him to the Grange. Still, the Archdeacon's letter to Carriston is a sufficient guarantee that he is not a swindler, so I will chance it.'

'I must now say good-bye,' said Caliphronas to the Rector, 'and thank you for your kindness. Of course I will see you soon again.'

'Oh yes.   You must come here as often as you can.'

'That will not be much if I am to sit for this artist,' laughed Caliphronas, turning to Maurice.   'Good-bye, sir ; I will see you to-night at six o'clock.'

He turned away gaily and left the garden, followed by the admiring glances of the two men, especially those of Maurice, who congratulated himself on his good fortune in obtaining such a perfect model.

Meanwhile, Caliphronas was walking swiftly in the direction of the Royland Arms.

'Good !' he muttered to himself in Greek.   'The first step is taken, so I have no fear now.'

CHAPTER V.

CRISPIN IS PUZZLED.

I've seen you before,
But where I forget,
Yet somewhere of yore,
I've seen you before;
You meet me once more,
A stranger—and yet
I've seen you before,
But where I forget.

UP and down the long terrace in front of the Grange walked Crispin, and, from the wrapt expression of his face, it would seem as though he were composing poetry ; but, as a matter of fact, he was thinking about Eunice. The course of their true love did not run smooth by any means, for Mrs. Dengelton, having found her daughter in the company of the poet, had marched off the former in order to lecture her about the latter. The substance, therefore, having been taken away, Crispin was left with only the shadow ; in other words, from speaking to Eunice, he was reduced to thinking of Eunice, which was not by any means so pleasant a position of affairs.

This uncomfortable state of things was due to the discovery made by Mrs. Dengelton, that her daughter had the previous evening been engaged in moon-gazing with the poet, a fact which the astute Parrot extracted with wonderful dexterity from her reluctant daughter. Mrs. Dengelton had talked a good deal about the family romance, as related to the Rector and Maurice, whereupon Eunice, having been asked questions concerning the same, was forced to admit that she had been absent during the recital. Her mother at once pounced down on this damaging admission like a hawk, and pressed the poor girl so mercilessly with questions, that she was obliged to tell of that pleasant half-hour on the terrace in company with Crispin.

On making this discovery, Mrs. Dengelton was too wise to reproach her daughter, and thereby run the risk of making her deaf to the voice of the charmer, *i.e.* resist her mother's desires in connection with matrimony. No, the elder lady said nothing about what she considered to be an act of madness, but privately determined to keep Crispin and Eunice apart by every means in her power. She was on the watch this morning, and, having finished the daily papers,—for Mrs. Dengelton prided herself on her universal knowledge of what was going on in the world,—went out to look for Eunice, who had disappeared. As she expected, she found her in the company of the poet, whereupon she made some ladylike excuse, — Mrs. Dengelton was an adept at telling white lies,—and took Eunice away to her room, where she kept her busy with letter-writing.

Crispin, therefore, deprived of the company of his inamorata, was by no means in a cheerful mood, and regretted that Eunice had not sufficient strength of mind to defy her mother, and end all his trouble by marrying him without delay. He had a very impulsive nature, and would have liked to sweep away these obstacles by sheer force of insistance that the marriage should take place at once; but his impulses were in a great measure restrained by experience in the school of the world, and he saw that it would be wiser to watch and wait. Already he was seriously thinking of ending his visit, and returning to town, in order to enlist his great friend, Lady Bentwitch, on his side, as such a fashionable personage might be able to talk Mrs. Dengelton into assenting to the marriage; but in spite of his strength of character he was reluctant to leave Eunice even for the short space of a week. So, like the ass between two bundles of hay, he could not quite make up his mind which course to take, when he saw Maurice coming leisurely along the terrace, and the conversation which ensued between them enabled him to at once settle his future movements.

When the master of Roylands reached his side, Crispin was struck with the unusual vivacity of his face. The gloomy look which it generally wore had quite disappeared, and in its place was an alert, eager expression, which showed that Maurice was deeply interested in some important matter.

'My dear Roylands,' cried Crispin in astonishment, 'why this transformation? Yesterday you were plunged in gloom, to-day Romeo on his way to Juliet looked not so happy. Who is the enchanter— or shall I say enchantress—who has worked this miracle?'

'The Rector has been giving me a lecture,' said Maurice gaily, lighting a cigarette; 'a terrible lecture, which reminded me of the days when I made false quantities in Latin verse, and translated good Greek into bad English.'

'Ah, you ought to have a lecture every day if it benefits you in this way. You are much pleasanter as Sancho Panza than as Don Quixote.'

'Explain!'

'Well, the squire was always merry, and the knight doleful; so I like you better as the former than as the latter.'

'I am afraid we have changed characters, Crispin. You are the Knight of the Rueful Countenance now.'

'Eunice'—

'*Cela va sans dire*,' said Maurice, leaning his elbows on the balustrade. 'Oh, do not look so astonished, Monsieur Cupid! I am not so blind but what I can see how things stand between you and Psyche.'

'You take credit to yourself when none is due,' replied Crispin significantly. 'Mr. Carriston drew your attention to our position. You did not see it for yourself.'

'That is true enough; but how did you guess that the Rector told me?'

'Because you were too much wrapped up in yourself to notice unhappy lovers.'

'Unhappy lovers?'

'Yes.   I love Eunice, and my affection is returned ;
but there is an obstacle which prevents our marriage.'

'And this obstacle?'

'Is yourself.'

'I?'

'You! Mrs. Dengelton wishes Eunice to marry
you.'

'There are always two to a bargain,' said Maurice
grimly. 'I don't want to marry Eunice.'

'Oh, you don't love her?'

'As a cousin, yes ; as a possible wife, no.'

'Then there is some chance for me?'

'I should say there was every chance for you,'
remarked Roylands in a friendly manner. 'You are
young and famous, you know every one, you go
everywhere, you are the adored of the gentle sex ; so
what more can Eunice or her mother desire?'

'Eunice desires nothing—except myself ; but as for
Mrs. Dengelton, she thinks I am poor.'

'Oh! and are you poor?'

'No ; on the contrary, I am very well off.'

'Then why don't you place all your perfections
before my dear aunt, and persuade her into consenting
to the match.'

'I don't want to do so—yet,' said Crispin, with some hesitation.

'Why all this mystery?'

'I cannot tell you just now, but you may be certain there is nothing wrong about the mystery. I will satisfy Mrs. Dengelton on all points shortly, and then, perhaps, I shall have the felicity of being your cousin-in-law.'

'I wish you good luck.'

'You would not object to my marrying your cousin?' asked Crispin timidly.

'I?' said Maurice in amazement. 'Certainly not! I believe in love matches; but, of course,—though I have but little to say in the matter,—I should like to know who you are, where you come from, and all that, before you become the husband of Eunice.'

'I will explain everything to your satisfaction—shortly.'

'The sooner the better for your own sake.'

'I don't understand you,' said Crispin, with some hauteur.

'I mean as regards Eunice,' explained Maurice quickly. 'If you don't tell my aunt of your intentions, and put yourself right as regards money and position in her eyes, she will marry Eunice to some one else. Failing me,—and I have not the slightest intention of marrying my dear cousin,—she will angle for another rich man, who will probably not be so blind to the charms of Eunice as I am. In that case, my poor Crispin, I am afraid it will be all up with you.'

'What you say is very true,' replied Crispin reflectively. 'I will speak to Mrs. Dengelton before I leave the Grange.'

'I cannot understand why you are making all this mystery.'

'Because I am proud,' rejoined the poet, with a flush on his dark cheek. 'I cannot explain myself now, but I will some day, and then you will see that I had a good reason for my reticence.'

'So be it. But at present you are a riddle.'

'Well, I suppose I am,' said Crispin smilingly; 'but one which will shortly be explained, and, like all riddles, turn out to be very disappointing. By the way, you might offer me one of those excellent cigarettes.'

'Certainly,' answered Maurice, holding out his open case. 'Unlike Caliphronas, you are fond of smoking.'

'Caliphronas! Who is he? what is it? man, woman, or child, or something to eat?'

'The first—a Greek. Count Constantine Cáliphronas.'

'Phœbus! what a name!' ejaculated Crispin, lighting his cigarette. 'Who is he?'

'A Greek nobleman.'

'Humph! I mistrust Greek noblemen.'

'Well, they have got a bad name,' said Maurice quite apologetically; 'but I don't think this one is a *chevalier d'industrie.*'

'The exception which proves the rule, perhaps,' replied Crispin idly; 'but really I have no right to call the Greeks names, as on the whole they are not bad. I have a good many friends among the countrymen of Plato.'

'Do you know Caliphronas?'

'Ah, that I cannot tell until I see him.'

'Well, you will see him soon, as he is coming to stay here for a few days.'

'Stay here!' said Crispin in some surprise. 'My dear Roylands, is not this a very sudden friendship?'

'It is not a friendship at all.'

'Well, when a man asks another to his house to stay—to be introduced to his relatives—it looks uncommonly like friendship.'

'I am not so conventional as most Englishmen,' said Maurice impatiently, 'and therefore do not act by rule. I daresay I should have made inquiries about the past of this Greek before asking him to my house; but, as far as that goes, you are a riddle yourself.'

Crispin's sallow cheek flushed at this home thrust, but he had great self-command, and replied quietly enough.

'That is rather a hard thing to say of me. I thought you were my friend.'

'Pardon me, old fellow,' said Roylands penitently. 'I did not mean to be so rude. I have an abominable temper, and should be kicked for saying such a thing in my own house.'

'I will let you off the kicking,' replied Crispin, recovering his good-humour. 'As you very truly say, I am a riddle; but I will explain myself soon. Still, this Count Caliphronas'—

'Do you know the name?'

'I have a faint idea of having heard it before.'

'In Greece?'

'Most probably. I know the isles of Greece very well.'

'Ah, is that a quotation from Byron, or a pointed

remark? In other words, is it a premeditated or a chance shot?'

'Surely chance—I only quoted from "Don Juan." Why do you ask?'

'Because this Count does come from the isles of Greece. He says he was born in Ithaca.'

'Ah, he is not reticent about himself,' said Crispin dryly. 'I will give you my opinion of the gentleman when I see him. At present I cannot recall the name precisely, though I fancy I have heard it before. Meanwhile, tell me all you know about him.'

'I am afraid that is but little. He arrived this morning at Roylands, with a letter of introduction to the Rector from the Archdeacon of Eastminster, and came to luncheon at the Rectory. During our conversation, he complained of how badly he was put up at the Royland Arms, and as I knew Carriston would ask him to stay at the Rectory, a thing I know he dislikes doing, as he hates strangers in his house, I took the bull by the horns, and asked Caliphronas to come here for a time. He accepted, and is to arrive with his traps this evening.'

'Was it merely for the sake of taking the burden off Mr. Carriston's shoulders that you gave your invitation?'

'Not entirely. This Caliphronas is a splendid-looking fellow, and I asked him to sit to me for my statue of Endymion.'

'Oh! is he worthy to be a model?'

'My dear Crispin, he has the most perfect figure for a man I ever saw in my life; wonderfully handsome, and with a wild, untamed air about him that is quite unique.'

Crispin listened to this speech without moving a muscle, but a strange look came into his eyes.

'Have you ever read *A Strange Story*, by Lytton?' he asked abruptly.

'Yes, several times,' replied Maurice, somewhat astonished at the irrelevancy of the question.

'Then does this man resemble Margrave, the hero of the book?'

'In what way?'

'In every way except the mysticism. Is he an ardent lover of Nature? Does he talk a lot about classical times? Is he impulsive and utterly selfish?'

'As to the last quality, I have not yet had an opportunity of judging, but for the rest, you have described him exactly.'

'Caliphronas!' murmured Crispin in a pondering manner.

'Do you know him?'

Crispin did not answer at once, and seemed to be making up his mind as to what he would say. At last he turned to Maurice with an enigmatic smile on his face, and shrugged his shoulders.

'Not so far as I can recollect. That description I have given as applied to Margrave, would suit a good many Greeks. They are mostly handsome, and especially so among the islands, for from living so much in the open air, they imbibe a great love for Nature. Naturally, as they have no modern glories to talk about, they boast of ancient times and ancient heroism. They are all impulsive, so you see I simply described the Greek at large, not this one in particular.'

'But you have described him exactly.'

'I tell you the description suits any Greek, as I have explained.'

'Then you don't know this man?'

'No; I know no one of the name of Caliphronas,' replied Crispin, with a slight emphasis on the last word.

Maurice did not notice the quibble, and with cheerful good-humour dismissed the subject from his mind, for, after all, this mystery, with which he enveloped the Count, might turn out to be but an unworthy suspicion. Plenty of Greeks come to England, and one more or less did not matter. He would trouble his head no more about this man who had dropped from the clouds into this dull little village, but make use of him as a model, and then say good-bye to him with the best grace in the world. Once he had left the Grange, it was unlikely he would ever cross his path again, as Maurice had not the slightest intention of going to Greece, and was looking forward to a humdrum life at Roylands for the next few years. How little did he know what was in store for him, and that from this appearance of Count Caliphronas was to date a new era in his life.

Meanwhile, Crispin, who in reality knew a good deal more than he chose to tell, was watching him keenly. 'You must not relapse into your gloomy fits again,' he said, laying his hand lightly on his friend's arm.

'I do not intend to,' replied Maurice cheerfully. 'No; I now see the excellence of the Rector's advice. Take an interest in life, and you will be happy. I am taking an interest in life—in your wooing of Eunice, and in Caliphronas.'

'Why Caliphronas?'

'Because he is my Endymion in the flesh. I am

going to create a wonderful statue, Crispin, the like of which has not been seen since the days of Canova. As to this riddle Caliphronas, we will solve him together.'

'Perhaps the solution may be easier than you think.

'Crispin, you know something about this man!'

'Nonsense! I tell you I know no one called Caliphronas.'

'Names may be assumed,' said Maurice shrewdly, 'and I am sure you have met the owner of this one before.'

'I meet so many people,' replied Crispin carelessly. 'It is probable I may have seen him; but really I can tell you nothing about him—yet.'

'Ah! then you will some day?'

'My dear Roylands,' said Crispin impatiently, 'Caliphronas and his past life is becoming quite a mania with you. I don't know the man, but, from your description, I fancy I have met with him, though, as I said before, such description would apply to dozens of other Levantine Greeks. When I see him I will tell you if I recognise him; but what then? he may only be a casual acquaintance, and his history quite unknown to me. If you mistrusted his looks, you should not have asked him to the Grange.'

'My dear fellow, it was on account of his looks I did ask him. He is my Endymion, remember. But you are right; I am making a mountain out of a molehill. Still, there is some excuse for me. A unique specimen of humanity like Caliphronas does not appear every day in a village like Roylands, so it is but natural I should be curious about him. But there, we will say no more about your brother mystery. I am going to have an interview with my bailiff, and you may thank your stars, my friend, you are a poet, and not a landed proprietor.'

Maurice sauntered away laughing, looking by no means the kind of man to overburden himself with work; but Crispin remained leaning over the balustrade of the terrace, gazing absently at the silver spray of the fountain glittering in the sunlight, and thought deeply.

'I wonder what he wants here,' thought the poet, with a frown on his expressive face. 'A man like that does not come down to a quiet village for nothing. Can it be to see me? No! that is impossible, as he could not know I am here. Curious I never saw him in London, for he must have been there at the same time as myself, unless, indeed, he has just arrived in England. That there is some scheme in his head, I am certain—if I could only see him alone and fathom his motives! Oh, you fox, you! Cunning as you are, I will foil you. It is no good you are after my friend, I'm sure of that.'

He walked forward a few paces, still pondering, then resumed his soliloquy in a muttered tone.

'Roylands said this Caliphronas was coming over about six o'clock. He is staying at the Royland Arms, so I think I will walk over there and see him; but no, that will attract attention, and I wish to tell Roylands nothing yet. I will send a note; no, that will not do. Ah! I have it. I will wait at the park gates and speak to him before he comes up to the house. No one will know, and I can find out the reason of his presence here.'

Decidedly this poet was a remarkably mysterious person, not only as concerned his own personality, but also as regards this brilliant stranger who was equally enigmatic. If Maurice found his life dull now, it evidently was not going to be so for any length of time; and, although he knew it not, the elements of romance had come into it in the most unexpected way in the persons of Crispin and Constantine Caliphronas.

Having thus made up his mind, the poet thought

no more about the Greek, but strolled round the side of the house to see if Eunice was at her window. He knew that Mrs. Dengelton especially affected a small boudoir in the left wing of the Grange, the window of which was only slightly raised above the terrace, and here Crispin felt sure Eunice would be. Fortunately for himself, he was right in his conjecture, for, on arriving in sight of the casement, he saw Eunice sitting at it in a dejected attitude, evidently expectant of a visit from her lover.

'Miss Dengelton!' he said cautiously, not knowing but what the dragon might be within hearing, and therefore adopting society manners.

'She has gone out of the room for a few minutes,' said his lady in a frightened whisper. 'Do go away.'

'What! when the coast is clear! Not if I know it.'

'I expect her back every minute.'

'Very well; till she arrives we can talk about ourselves, and even when she does we can surely chat about the weather.'

'I heard you laughing with Maurice.'

'Yes; he is quite gay to-day. He has found a model for his statue of Endymion.'

'Some village bumpkin?'

'No, a Greek gentleman.'

'A Greek! and pray what is a Greek doing down here?'

Crispin shrugged his shoulders.

'I'm sure I don't know. You will see him to-night, so don't fall in love with him.'

'Why should I?'

'He is very handsome.'

'I don't care for handsome men, they are so conceited.'

'Humph! that is not a compliment to me.'

'Well, you are not conceited, are you?'

'Nor handsome.'

'You are handsome enough for me, at all events,' said Eunice coquettishly.

'What a charming compliment!' replied Crispin gaily; 'for that I will give you a rose.'

'Hush! here comes my mother.'

But Crispin, alas! had not heard the warning, and, having plucked the finest rose he could see, returned to the window, to find himself confronted by the gaudy figure of The Parrot, whose beady eyes sparkled maliciously as he approached.

'What! a rose for me, dear Mr. Crispin?' she said, stretching out her hand, in which Crispin was unwillingly compelled to place his flower; 'how kind of you! The young men of to-day are gallant after all. Look, Eunice, is not this flower charming? almost as charming as you are, Mr. Crispin. The Rose of Sharon—oh, Shiraz—you see I've read your book. Now, I have no time to talk, my dear Mr. Crispin, so you must go away for the present at all events. We shall meet at luncheon, and if you are very good you may bring me in another rose.'

Mrs. Dengelton, having thus vanquished the enemy, disappeared with her daughter and shut the window, upon which poor Crispin walked away in a rage.

'Old cat!' he said, which was certainly neither polite nor poetical.

CHAPTER VI.

SUB ROSÂ.

Secrets absurd
Leading to woes,
Only are heard
Under the rose.

Maidens refuse,
Lovers propose,
Just as they choose,
Under the rose.

How scandals spread
Nobody knows,
For they are said
Under the rose.

WHEN anything marvellous occurs in real life, wiseacres shake their heads, and say, 'Wonderful! extraordinary! Truth is stranger than fiction.' But when a novel contains any incident out of the common, these same inconsistent people refuse to believe it, on the plea that

'Fiction is not stranger than truth.' They entirely forget that fiction is but a reflection of real life, and that man can imagine nothing, but merely reproduces what he sees around him. The sceptic will object,—'Fairy tales!' Well, my dear doubter, how do you know that fairy tales do not contain a germ of truth? there may have been fairies in the earlier ages of the world, and if so, the chronicles of Fairyland are as authentic as those of England—perhaps more so, seeing all histories are tinctured more or less with partizanship.

Who would have believed in the mammoth, had not the huge beast been reconstructed by Cuvier? or in the moa, had not the skeleton of that gigantic bird been discovered in New Zealand? Nay, there is doubtless much truth in those extravagant travels of Marco Polo, Sir John Mandeville, and such-like wanderers. The middle ages were the times of improbability, not of impossibility, for but little was known of the geographical world.

Well, we of this nineteenth century have discovered all possible continents, and assume that we know everything; but such is not the case, for, though we may have exhausted the geographical world, we know comparatively few of the secrets of Nature. The pebble parable of Sir Isaac Newton will here occur to many minds, and it applies as truly to our times as to his own. Earth, sky, and water are full of secrets, many of which yet defy our efforts to learn and catalogue them. This century has been prolific of discoveries, but even add another hundred years of fresh revelations, and Nature will still give us riddles to solve out of her exhaustless store.

Therefore, when a coincidence occurs in a fiction, though it may be improbable, it is not impossible, and he who takes the trouble to keep his eyes open, his mental as well as his physical eyes, will, in nearly every case, find the counterpart of the ideal in the real. Here, then, are two mysterious individuals, who, masquerading under the names of Crispin and Caliphronas, meet one another in the most un-expected manner in the most unexpected place. Wiseacres will at once say 'Impossible!' but, going on the theory set forth as before, such a meeting is not only possible, but probable. Fate, Destiny, Fortune, —whatever be the name of the power which guides our circumstances,— delights in surprises quite as much as does the novelist; therefore, why should we believe the first and doubt the second? This is inconsistent! Therefore, if you who read are wise in your generation, and broad in your views of probability, you will see nothing impossible in this unexpected meeting of poet and adventurer.

Caliphronas was an adventurer pure and simple, that is, of course, as regards his vocation as free lance, but not as touching his moral or physical qualities. He had come to England with a distinct end in view, and had already made the first step towards the accomplishment of that end. Whether his intentions were good or bad remains to be seen, and if, my dear reader, you cannot tell the quality of his designs from the character of the man as before described, you must perforce remain in ignorance, even as Crispin remained, for, truth to tell, that astute individual was for once in his life really and truly puzzled. He had known Caliphronas in Greek waters, under another name, and, having had considerable experience of his character, was quite confident that he had some object in view for thus making his appearance at Roylands. With the determination of finding out that object, and thwarting it if he could, —for Crispin had no very great love for the Greek, —our poet walked down to the park gates between the hours of five and six, with the intention of having an interview with this mysterious stranger.

In his own mind he was by no means certain of the identity of this Caliphronas with the person he thought he was, and such a doubt could only be solved by a personal view of the Greek himself; but the description given by Maurice so tallied with the image of a certain individual, that Crispin felt sure that the conclusion he had arrived at was a correct one. In order, however, to end all doubt on the subject, he wished to personally interview the Count before he set foot in Roylands Grange, and had with considerable dexterity carried out his plan without exciting suspicion, a thing which he was anxious to avoid if possible.

Pleading a headache,—that convenient excuse,—he had managed to give his friend the slip, though, truth to tell, he took more trouble over securing such secrecy than was absolutely necessary, for Maurice, fired by the idea of recommencing work, had retreated to his studio, and remained there all the afternoon. Mrs. Dengelton still kept a watchful eye upon her daughter, and, on one plea or another, kept her away from the too-fascinating poet; so, in reality, Crispin was left entirely to his own devices, and thereupon utilized such good fortune by seeking this important interview with the unknown Greek.

So hot had been the day, that Crispin felt a
certain sense of relief when the coolness of night
approached, and, lingering under the mighty oaks
which bordered the avenue, he luxuriated in that
delightful twilight, which is neither wholly of night
or day, but partakes equally of both. The air was still
warm, and there was a pleasant shade over the sky,
as Night gradually drew her dusky veil across the
glaring blue from east to west. Shafts of crimson
light shot through the wood, and through the dense
foliage Crispin could see at times the rosy flames
of the setting sun. Still vocal were the birds, for
they were now singing their good-night to day, and
in a short time nothing would be heard but occasional
chirps from some belated thrush, until with the moon
came the divine nightingale to flood the thickets
with song. Restless gnats were dancing in front of
his face as he strolled down the avenue, and at
times a bat would flit noiselessly through the warm
air, while, mellowed by distance, the chimes of
Roylands church rang musically on his ear.

'Six o'clock,' said the poet to himself, glancing
at his watch, 'I suppose this Caliphronas will be
here shortly. Roylands sent the dogcart, but if
this is the man I imagine, he will send on his traps

in charge of the groom, and walk over to the Grange on such a perfect evening.'

At this moment he heard the noise of approaching wheels, and shortly afterwards the dogcart, drawn by a fast-trotting mare, flashed past him, containing only the groom and some luggage. Finding his conjecture thus prove correct, Crispin did not trouble himself to go further on his way to seek Caliphronas, as that gentleman was bound to meet him in the avenue; so, lounging against the mighty trunk of an oak, he lazily waited the approach of the individual concerning whose intentions he entertained such doubts.

> *' I will crown myself with roses*
> *To meet thee, beloved.*
> *Why dost thou fly at the sight of my wreath?*
> *The hot sun hath withered it truly.*
> *And my heart is burnt up by thine eyes.*
> *Dead heart! dead roses! but love undying!'*

Caliphronas was singing these words in Greek, and Crispin at once recognised the voice of the singer, a recognition which immediately confirmed his suspicions as to the identity of this gentleman.

> *' We will live in the woods, my beloved,*
> *And berries will be our food;*
> *On berries and kisses could I live always.*
> *Till Fate destroyed us,*
> *And robbed us of berries, and kisses, and life, for ever.*

'I've heard him sing that song at Melnos,' muttered Crispin quietly to himself. 'It is he! What can he be doing here?'

At this moment the singer came in sight, walking rapidly up the avenue with a springy step, swinging his stick to and fro as he sang. He was indeed a sight worth looking at, as he bounded lightly over the earth, Antæus-like, drawing fresh vigour at every pressure of his foot on the ground; yet his undeniable beauty but excited a feeling of repulsion in the breast of Crispin, who now knew him only too well. They formed a strange contrast, these two men; the poet small, dark, and unhandsome, but the fire of intellect in his eyes; the adventurer a splendid animal, with nothing but his physical perfections to recommend him.

Caliphronas did not notice the poet leaning against the tree, and came on, carelessly singing as he walked—

> *'What will I do for thee, beloved?*
> *Oh, I will do many deeds of daring!*
> *I will slay the Turk in his pride,*
> *And his head will be my wedding gift.*
> *Behold I'*—

Here he stopped suddenly, catching sight of Crispin, but, instead of being astonished at the unexpected meeting, as the poet expected, he simply stood still, leaning on his stick, and laughing at the look on the other's face.

'Ah, ah, Crispin!' he said in Greek, with a smile; 'you did not expect to see me in this place.'

'Certainly I did not,' retorted Crispin in the same language, marvelling at the self-possession of the man; 'and I've no doubt the meeting is unexpected on both sides.'

'Not with me; oh no! That priest—the Papa I saw this morning told me you were here, and your friend also informed me of your presence.'

'What are you doing here?'

'Ah, that is a long story, my good Crispin,' replied Caliphronas coolly, 'and one I do not choose to tell.'

'You have some design in your head.'

'Assuredly,' said the Count mockingly; 'I would not come to this cold island for pleasure.'

'Ah, I see you are as great a scoundrel as ever!'

Caliphronas laughed, and seemed in nowise offended at the scornful tone of the other. For such an epithet an Englishman would have struck its utterer, but Caliphronas did not even frown. The only notice he took of Crispin's rudeness was to raise his eyebrows in mocking surprise.

'You have still a bad opinion of me, I see.'

'The very worst!'

'What a truly good young man you are!' said the Count sardonically. 'I regret that you should be forced to associate with such a scamp as I am; but I am afraid you will have to make up your mind to that, or—go away.'

'I shall certainly not do the latter until I find out the reason of your presence in this place.'

'Then, my dear friend, you will have to stay here for ever.'

'Are you going to stay here for ever?'

'I! no. I am down here on business.'

'With the Rector? — with Roylands? — with whom?'

The Count looked at him with a provoking smile, and flung himself on the grass at the foot of the oak against which Crispin was leaning.

'Perhaps with both ; perhaps with neither.'

'Now you listen to me, Caliphronas,—as that is the name you choose to go by: both Mr. Carriston and Mr. Roylands are friends of mine, and if you have come down here with any bad design in your head against either of them, I will make it my business to thwart you.'

'Do so by all means, if you can.'

'I can do so by a very simple means, though you seem to doubt it,' said Crispin quietly. 'You brought an excellent letter of introduction to Mr. Carriston, though how you came by it I do not know. You have made friends with Roylands, who is a simple fellow, by consenting to be his model for Endymion '—

'And a very good model too,' interrupted Caliphronas, looking at himself complacently.

'I don't deny your outward goodliness ;—it is a pity your mind is not in keeping. But to come back to what I was saying. You have made friends with both the gentlemen I speak of, and perhaps such friendship is necessary to your plans; if so, I will end it.'

'How will you manage that?' said the Count coolly, but with a nasty glitter in his eyes.

'Simply by telling them who you are and what you are.'

'You will not do that!'

'I will, if your designs are bad.'

'How do you know my designs are bad?'

'Because to a man of your nature goodness is impossible.'

'I would not go so far as to say it is impossible,' said Caliphronas, with a sneer, 'but I agree with you that it is improbable. To my mind, goodness is a weakness.'

'One you don't possess, I'm afraid.'

'I do not; nor do I wish to possess it,' replied the Count insolently. 'But may I draw your attention to the fact that it is long past six, that Roylands dines at seven, and that I am terribly hungry?'

'You can call my attention to all these facts,' retorted Crispin promptly, 'but you don't enter that house until I know what you are going to do.'

'Pay a visit. Sit for the Endymion.'

'I am tired of this fencing. Don't go on like this with me, An'—

'Caliphronas,' said the other quickly.

'Well, one name is as good as another; but you needn't waste all this diplomacy on me, my friend. I know you too well to believe you would waste your time in coming here for nothing. Now tell me what your schemes are, or I will reveal all I know of you to Maurice Roylands.'

The Count being thus driven into a corner, all his suavity of manner vanished as he sat up on the turf with a scowl on his handsome face, and a significant movement of his right hand towards his waist.

'Oh, I'm not afraid of that, you scamp,' said Crispin quickly ; 'you wear not the fusanella here, nor have you knife or pistol with you. You are in a civilised country, my noble Count, so must act in a civilised manner.'

The Greek, recovering his temper, burst out laughing, and beckoned Crispin to sit down beside him on the soft green turf.

'You have the whip-hand of me, Crispin,' he said lightly ; 'and I am too wise a man to waste time in argument, so I will tell you the reason of my presence here. You were quite right in thinking I did not come for pleasure ; on the contrary, I wish to carry out a very delicate affair, and perhaps it is as well you should know, as I may want your assistance in the matter.'

'I will help you in none of your villainies.'

'By St. Theodore, how pious you have become ! Oh, I forgot ! you are Mister Crispin, the famous poet, the new Chrysostom of the Golden Mouth. Eh yes ; I heard all about you in London. No one would think this great poet was ever '—

' Hold your tongue !' said Crispin, roughly grasping the Greek by the wrist ; ' whatever I have been, whatever I am, I have done nothing to be ashamed of.'

' Indeed ! would you like them to know all ?' retorted the Count, jerking his hand in the direction of the house.'

' I intend to tell them all when I choose ; but not before.'

' Suppose I anticipate you ?'

' Do so, by all means.   You will relate the story of my life, and I will relate the story of your life.   I wonder which will prove the most interesting.'

' Oh, I wonder,' rejoined Caliphronas, with consummate impudence ; ' but do not let us quarrel, as I may want your assistance.   Oh, you need not frown ; I have no ill intentions towards your precious friends.   In fact, to put you completely at your ease, I may as well tell you Justinian sent me to England.'

' Justinian !' repeated Crispin, with a start.   ' Well, what of that ?' he resumed carelessly.   ' You know I am not now friends with Justinian,—I have not seen him for nearly '—

' Three years, eh ?' said Caliphronas quickly ; ' of course, that is just about the time you came here. Oh, I heard all about you in London ; and Justinian will have heard also by this time, for I wrote and told him all.'

'I trust he is pleased,' said Crispin grimly.

'As to that, I don't know. True, his goose has turned out a swan, and now, unlike a swan, sings songs the world listens to ; but such glory can hardly compensate him for the ungrateful manner in which you treated him.'

'Enough!' cried Crispin hotly, his dark face flushing with anger ; 'I can justify my conduct amply, but I do not choose to do so to you. Leave Justinian, and Melnos, and all the old life alone. I want to know the reason of your presence in Roylands.'

'Well, you shall know. But do not get furious over nothing, said Caliphronas mockingly. 'I am afraid you have lost all your old Hellenic calm, and now resemble one of these bad-tempered Englishmen, devoured with the spleen, and greedy of money.'

'I am not greedy of money.'

'Eh ? oh, I see! you sing your songs for the smiles of women, not for the gold of their husbands, fathers, and brothers. Well, I agree with you ; the smiles of women are very delightful, but one cannot live on them, so I would like to know how you exist.'

'Would you, indeed ?'

' Yes; and so would Justinian.'

' Well, you will neither of you be told. Come now, it is growing late, and I wait for your confession.'

' No one will hear us?'

' Of course not; besides, we speak in Greek, which is not so common in England as in Hellas.'

Caliphronas let the smile die away from his lips, and looked keenly at Crispin.

' You will not reveal what I have now to tell you?'

' Not unless it is some villainy.'

' It is no villainy. It is an act of justice. Listen.'

The story, which did not take long to tell, drew forth many exclamations of surprise from Crispin, who for once in his life was astonished at the revelations of Caliphronas, and believed he was speaking the truth. Indeed, he could hardly help believing it, as many points of the story coincided with what he himself knew in connection with the Roylands family. When Caliphronas had finished his recital, he flung himself back on the turf, and waited for Crispin to speak, which the young man did after a long pause.

' What you have stated astonishes me very much,' he said deliberately; ' but, so far as I can see, there does not seem to be any harm intended to my friend.'

'None in the least,' said the Count eagerly. 'You do not like Justinian now, for some mysterious reason, but I think you know enough about him to trust him.'

'I know enough about him not to trust him over-much,' replied Crispin coolly ; 'but with regard to your scheme and his scheme '—

'Yes?' cried the Count breathlessly.

'I will remain neutral.'

Caliphronas drew a long breath of relief, and sprang to his feet.

'That is better than nothing ; but I wish you would help me.'

'No ; I will remain neutral.'

'You can see for yourself there is no harm in-tended.'

'I tell you I will remain neutral,' said Crispin for the third time, also rising from his recumbent atti-tude. 'I will neither help you nor thwart you ; so you can do as you please, but I don't think you'll succeed in your schemes.'

'Don't you?' replied Caliphronas provokingly, as they walked up to the house together. 'Well, that remains to be seen. If a man of my capacity '—

'Cunning.'

'Well, cunning if you like. If a man of my cunning cannot circumvent this dull-headed '—

'Cautious.'

'Oh, is he cautious? Well, I will make this cautious Englishman do as I wish. But here we are nearly at the house, and I wait to know on what footing we stand.'

'You are an acquaintance of mine. I met you at Athens. Talk of the best-known Athenians as our mutual friends.'

'And you will say nothing about Melnos?'

'No.'

'Nor about Justinian?'

'No.'

'Nor Alcibiades?'

'I tell you I won't say a word about any one or anything,' said Crispin impatiently. 'You can carry out your plan if you like. It does no harm to Roylands so far as I can see; but if I find you playing double, my friend, I'll put an end to your games.'

'I always play fair when it is to my benefit to do so,' retorted the Greek, with an unpleasant smile.

'What a pity it is not always to your benefit to do so!' said the poet cruelly; 'you would then be an honest man.'

'I am what I am,' answered Caliphronas sullenly;
'had I created myself, I might have made an improve-
ment.'

'Not in your appearance,' observed Crispin, looking
at the splendid beauty of the man beside him. 'I
suppose you are as vain as ever?'

'Possibly; but I never let my vanity interfere with
my business.'

'Ah, there is some sense in that handsome head of
yours, but precious little.'

'Quite enough to accomplish my wishes.'

'I doubt it. However, here we are, and here is Mr.
Roylands.'

It was indeed Maurice, who, arrayed in evening
dress, advanced to meet them, and greeted Caliphronas with a smile.

'I had quite given you up, Count,' he said, shaking
hands with the Greek; 'your luggage arrived, but
not you, and the dinner is now due. However, as
neither of you gentlemen are ready, I have put it
off for half an hour, so you will just have time to
dress. You know Mr. Crispin, Count?'

'Yes; you must blame him for my unpunctuality,'
said Caliphronas gracefully. 'I walked over here,
and sent on my luggage by your groom. In the

avenue I met Mr. Crispin, and we talked of old times.'

'Ah, you know one another!' cried Maurice, flashing a keen glance at Crispin, which that gentleman sustained without blenching.

'Oh yes,' answered the poet calmly; 'I was afraid I did not know the name of Count Caliphronas, but my memory played me false. I know it and him very well. We met at Athens.'

'Three years ago,' continued the Count, laughing. 'You have no idea, Mr. Maurice, how astonished I was to meet my friend here. By the way, you must allow me to call you Mr. Maurice; I make such a mess of your English names.'

'I think you speak English wonderfully well, Count. Where did you learn, may I ask, if it is not a rude question?'

'I had an English tutor,' replied Caliphronas, stealing a glance at Crispin; 'and I have been accustomed to your tongue since a lad.'

'Ah, that accounts for it. Well, come with me, Count, and I will show you your room. Crispin, Mrs. Dengelton and her daughter are already in the drawing-room, so you had better make haste.'

Crispin went off as quickly as possible, and Maurice

hospitably conducted his guest to the room prepared for him, where Roylands' valet was already spreading out the Count's evening dress. This duty having been performed, Mr. Roylands hurried away to his guests in the drawing-room, and the Count was left alone with the valet, whom he speedily dismissed.

'Thank you; I shan't require anything else,' he said, when the servant had arranged all his clothes. 'I am accustomed to wait on myself. Dinner is in half an hour?'

'Yes, sir,' replied the valet, and retired quietly.

The fact is, Caliphronas had a habit of thinking aloud, and, as he had a good many matters to consider, he was afraid of committing himself if a second person were in the room; therefore, having got rid of the servant, he began to dress slowly for dinner, thinking deeply all the time.

'I do not think Crispin will say anything,' he said aloud in Greek, as he arranged his white tie; 'very likely he will help me, if I can manage him. How upright he is now—how very upright, and to think'—

Here the Count went into a fit of silent laughter, which lasted until he arrived at the door of the drawing-room, when he controlled his risible muscles, and went in gravely to be introduced to the ladies.

CHAPTER VII.

SOUVENT FEMME VARIE.

Woman's a weathercock,
Full of frivolity ;
Men may together mock
At her heart's quality.
But if a heart she steals,
Worth all the smart she feels,
There then her place is ;
Lo, then the nether rock
Less firm of base is.

EEDLESS to say, Count Constantine Caliphronas was much admired by the two
ladies, which was scarcely to be wondered
at, seeing his charm of manner was almost as great
as his physical perfection. Attracted in the first
instance by his good looks, they were quite prepared
to find the kernel of such a handsome nut somewhat
disappointing ; in other words, they fancied that
Nature could scarcely be so profuse in her gifts, as to

give this man great mental powers in addition to his comely exterior. To their surprise, they found the Greek to be a charming conversationalist, and were much astonished at the purity with which he spoke the English tongue.

It would be ridiculous to say that Caliphronas was a man of any great intellectual powers; for, as before stated, he was gifted with more cunning than brains, still, such cunning enabled him to conceal his educational deficiencies, and by a dexterous use of the little knowledge he possessed, he managed to pass for a very intelligent man. Shallow Caliphronas was, without doubt, and his education in many ways had been woefully neglected ; but he had travelled a great deal, he was acute enough in picking up unconsidered trifles of general information, he had plenty of small talk, so all these advantages, in conjunction with his undeniable good looks and ready wit, enabled him to fascinate the ordinary run of people. A clever man or a brilliant woman would have discovered the smallness of his intellectual powers at once ; but everyday folk are not so difficult to please, and both Mrs. Dengelton and her daughter, being ordinary folk, gifted with ordinary brains, found the flashy, frivolous chatter of the Count infinitely charming.

Maurice, having got over his first suspicions of
the Greek, soon liked him extremely, as he was a
pleasant companion, and always in a good humour.
On the other hand, Crispin, who knew what Caliphronas really was, and how mean and vile a soul
inhabited that splendid body, was much put to in
order to conceal his distaste for the society of this
brilliant stranger.   He saw through the thin veneer
of good manners and facile accomplishments, into the
true nature of the man, and was well aware that this
apparently charming child of Nature, all impulse and
simplicity, was in reality a crafty, selfish, sensual
scoundrel, whose only aim in life was to benefit
himself at the expense of others.

'If we were only in the Palace of Truth now!'
thought the poet, as he sat silently watching the
dexterous way in which Caliphronas was using his
small stock of accomplishments. 'I wonder what
they would say were that man compelled to give
utterance to his real thoughts.   They would fly in
horror from him as a vile thing, a beautiful flower,
whose appearance is exquisite, yet whose odour is
death.   Still, he has improved wonderfully since the
old days.   I wonder where he picked up these good
manners—not from Justinian or Alcibiades, I'll be

bound; but perhaps he has been learning the art of pleasing from Helena.'

As this thought came into his mind, and he remembered the charming woman who bore that name, knowing what Caliphronas was, he could not restrain a shudder, which immediately drew the eyes of the Greek towards him.

'Eh, my friend Mr. Crispin,' he said slowly, you shudder! Some one is walking over your grave.'

'Oh, what a horrible idea!' cried Mrs. Dengelton in her liveliest manner, for the Count's good looks had made a deep impression on her elderly heart. 'I declare, my dear Count, you make me shudder also. It is exactly the kind of thing my brother Rudolph would say. Ghouls, vampires, omens, dreams, and all those gruesome things, he used to revel in. Yes, positively revel in. Never shall I forget being told how he brought some lady friend a book to read, called *Footprints on the Borders of another World*. It nearly frightened her into convulsions, and she threw it out of the window.'

'My Uncle Rudolph must have been an interesting kind of person,' said Maurice dryly.

'Oh, my dear Maurice, he was so terribly wild!

Yes! Why, in the old days, he would have been a buccaneer or a pirate—it is just the kind of thing he would have liked to have been.'

At this last remark, Crispin looked straight at the Count, who met his gaze with an uneasy laugh, and tried to turn the conversation.

'This gentleman, madam? He was very adventurous, I presume?'

'Oh dear me, yes! Your uncle, Eunice, I am speaking of—your uncle, Maurice.'

'Yes, mamma—yes, aunt,' said both the cousins together.

'He had a fiery eye, and was over six feet in height. I always thought him the image of the Templar in *Ivanhoe;* but, of course, I speak from hearsay, as I was a babe when he left England. Is there not a portrait of him somewhere, Maurice?'

'It is just behind you, aunt, over the piano.'

Both Caliphronas and Crispin arose with a simultaneous movement, and strolled across the room to look at this modern Captain Kidd, for that style of man he appeared to have been, judging from Mrs. Dengelton's highly-coloured description.

The portrait was a full-length one of a handsome

young fellow in the old-fashioned costume *à la d'Orsay* of the early Victorian age, and assuredly he appeared to be a dandy of the first water. But his strong commanding face, his eagle glance, firm mouth, and prominent nose marked him at once as a born leader of men. A man who, in Elizabethan times, would have sailed the Spanish Main and thrashed the Dons; who, in later years, would have delighted in Jacobite conspiracies; who would have fought his way to a marshal's baton when Napoleon led the armies of France: in fact, one of those men who find no outlet for their energies in the leading-strings of civilisation, but who, in a lawless life, develop those qualities whereof heroes are made. Maurice was good-looking enough in an ordinary fashion, but he had none of that power and daring in his face, such as showed so conspicuously in his uncle's countenance.

The Count and Crispin remained looking at the portrait an unconscionably long time, considering the original was unknown to them, and glanced meaningly at one another as they went back to their seats.

'Your description is an admirable one, Mrs. Dengelton,' said Crispin, as that lady evidently desired his opinion of the portrait; 'the face is that of a man who would be either a hero or a scoundrel according to circumstances, but always brave.'

'My dear Mr. Crispin!' cried the lady, somewhat scandalized at the epithet applied to a Roylands.

'I beg your pardon, Mrs. Dengelton; I am speaking of the type more than the man. Rudolph Roylands has the bearing of a born leader of men, and I do not wonder he left England for wider fields. He must have been stifled in this narrow island.'

'How do you know he left England?' asked the lady sharply.

'Why, your story of last night'—

'But you were not here when I told it. Ah, my dear Mr. Crispin, I am indeed very angry at you for taking my daughter out on to the terrace. She might have caught her death of cold—but we will not speak of that. At all events, you could not have heard my story.'

Crispin looked rather uncomfortable, as if he feared he had committed himself; but, as Mrs. Dengelton's beady eyes were fastened shrewdly on his face, he had to make some answer, though, truth to tell, he did not know what to say.

'Well, really, Mrs. Dengelton, I hardly know how to reply,' he said, colouring. 'I did not hear all your story; but, if you remember, just before the Rector said good-night, you talked about your brother leaving England.'

'Dear me, yes, so I did!' said Mrs. Dengelton, and she would have liked to have added something anent the story of the photographs, the falsehood of which she had discovered. Maurice, however, guessed how the land lay, and feeling sorry for Crispin, who was really very uncomfortable, made the first remark that came into his head. Caliphronas, tired of the conversation, had gone to the piano, where Eunice was playing softly, and talked to her in an undertone. This attention, however was not noticed by Crispin, who was too busy trying to extricate himself from his dilemma with Mrs. Dengelton, to think of anything else. How he would have managed to evade the photograph question, which Mrs. Dengelton was bent on asking, it is difficult to say, but that Maurice came to his aid with the apparently irrelevant remark,—

'My dear Crispin, you say that, judging from his face, my uncle would either be a hero or a scoundrel. Now what do you mean by that remark?'

'Oh, I hope I haven't offended you by making it,'

said Crispin, with a grateful smile, for he saw through Roylands' stratagem; 'but if a man like your uncle has, strongly developed, such qualities as he seems to possess, they are bound to break out in some direction. Place him in the army, and he will be a hero in time of war, but supposing he was born in Whitechapel, I am afraid his heroic qualities would be dangerous to society.'

'Then you think a hero and a thief are composed of the same qualities.'

'I will not say a thief, but use the milder term, "adventurer." If the great Napoleon had not been an adventurer of that quality, he would never have mounted the throne of France. Sforza, the Duke of Milan, was of the same species; so was William the Conqueror, and Roger de Hauteville, King of Sicily. All these men, through force of circumstances which aided the development of their commanding qualities, obtained thrones—they were adventurers who became kings. On the other hand, look at Benvenuto Cellini. He had the same instincts for fighting, commanding, and daring, the same longing for fame, riches, adventures; yet, to the end of his life, he was but a quarrelsome swashbuckler, simply because his circumstances did not permit of his qualities developing in the right direction. Cromwell had these qualities and mounted a throne, Rienzi had them and died on the scaffold—all through force of circumstance. Believe me, my dear Maurice, whatever qualities a man may possess, the development of them in the right or the wrong direction depends on his surroundings. It is a common saying that genius can override all obstacles —a mistake which any one who reads history can perceive. Circumstances are sometimes too strong for the greatest soul, and that genius which should have created empires dies in obscurity.'

'Quite a historical lecture, I declare,' tittered Mrs. Dengelton, who found this long speech a trifle wearisome ; ' but how does all this apply to my brother ? '

'If your brother, Mrs. Dengelton, went to South America, he probably rose to be president of one of those petty republics ; if he went as a free lance into the service of some Eastern potentate, he very likely ended his life as a pasha of three tails ; but if he stayed in England, I feel certain that his violent temperament, his adventurous longings, must have brought him into trouble.'

' I don't think he stayed in England,' replied Mrs. Dengelton, shaking her head, ' or we certainly should have heard of his death. Probably he is a president, or a pasha, or some of those dreadful things you speak of.'

'Do you think he is dead, aunt?' asked Maurice, who had been listening quietly to this argument.

'I'm sure I don't know. I haven't heard of him for years and years; but the Roylands are always long-living people, so perhaps he is still alive. It is now fifty years since he went away, at the age of twenty-five, so if he is still alive he must be quite seventy-five years of age.'

'Seventy-five years of age,' repeated Crispin, and relapsed into silence.

'Who is seventy-five years of age?' asked Cali-phronas, overhearing the remark.

'My Uncle Rudolph, if alive,' said Maurice lazily.

'Oh, indeed!' replied Caliphronas carelessly, but his words conveyed volumes as he tried to catch the eye of Crispin. In this, however, he was not success-ful, as Crispin was wrapt up in a brown study, so the Greek turned towards Eunice and asked her to sing something.

'I am passionately fond of music,' he said, turning over some songs, 'and nothing so delights me as to hear a woman's voice.'

Eunice blushed at this compliment to her sex, and,

not knowing how to answer it,—for she was still
afflicted with the shyness of the bread-and-butter
age,—took up the first song that came to hand.

'Do you know this song?' she said, placing the
music before her,—'"The Star Sirius;" it is the
new scientific style of song, now all the rage.'

'A scientific song,' repeated Caliphronas, rather
puzzled.

'Yes; blending instruction with pleasure,' said
Crispin, rousing himself out of his reverie and
walking over to the piano. 'The public are tired
of love-songs, sea-songs, sacred songs, comic songs,
and sentimentalities of all kinds; so some ingenious
person has invented the scientific song. In this song
astronomy is brought to the aid of eroticism, and the
result is peculiar, to say the least of it. I presume
such ditties are written for musically-inclined Girton
girls. Shall I play your accompaniment, Miss
Dengelton?'

'If you would be so kind,' said Eunice, vacating
her seat at the piano, which action brought a frown
to the face of her watchful mother. 'I can sing
better standing up.'

Crispin played the prelude in sufficiently good
style, and Caliphronas, sinking into a chair near

the singer, looked up into her face in a somewhat bold fashion, as she sang the latest up-to-date song of the day.

THE STAR SIRIUS.

I.

A glowing star of ardent ray
  In midnight skies we trace,
It is a central sun, they say,
  Enshrined in distant space.
Around it giant planets turn,
  In motion constant roll,
With fiery force its splendours burn,
  As for thee burns my soul.
Oh, star ascendant at my birth!
For tears, for sadness, or for mirth,
You rule my destiny on earth.

II.

Oh, star of stars! in thee no flaw
  The telescopes reveal;
Thine orbs obey attraction's law,
  And round thy centre wheel.
Beloved, thou and I are one,
  Nor parted e'er can be;
I am thy planet, thou my sun,
  For all eternity.
Oh, star ascendant at my birth!
For tears, for sadness, or for mirth,
You rule my destiny on earth.

'Thank you, Miss Dengelton,' said Caliphronas, when the song ended; 'I like your singing much better than the words. They are somewhat perplexing.'

'They are up-to-date words,' remarked Crispin calmly; 'the music is also up to date, of the most advanced school, a blending of Dvořák and Rubinstein.'

'What awful names!' cried Caliphronas, with a shudder; 'they grate on the ear.'

'So does their music in some cases; there is nothing like consistency. Still, some of the advanced school of music's efforts are delightful. This dance of Dvořák's, for instance.'

Bringing down his hands on the keys with a crash, he played one of those weird gipsy dances of the Bohemian musician, which thrill the listener with their wild capriciousness, and conjure up pictures of a mode of life quite alien to our prosaic respectability. That strange chord resounds loudly through the room, and at once we see the wild horses flying across the illimitable grey plain, and hear the fierce voices of their gipsy riders pealing up to the sombre sky of midnight. That rapid medley of sounds, and lo! the fires burn redly under the trees, while round them bound tawny women with flashing eyes, tossing their arms and clashing their tambourines to the wild rhythm of the music. Death on the cards, love in the stars, and the muttered prophecies of crouching hags, terrified at the omen of flying bat, of shrieking night-bird. Another whirl of glittering notes scatter themselves through the air, crash, crash, crash, chord upon chord sounds fiercely, with intervals of sparkling chromatic runs like the falling of broken spray, and then one final chord, bringing the red of the dawn, the chill winds of morning, and the uprising of the cheerful sun.

'Wonderful!' cried Mrs. Dengelton, who knew nothing about music, but admired Dvořák because he was the fashion, and not intelligible to the ordinary mind.

'So fantastic,' added Eunice, whose accomplishments did not soar above the mild singing of a mild drawing-room ballad, such as 'Daddy's Dancing,' or 'Oh, if to thee my heart is welcome!'

'Well, for my part,' said the Count, shrugging his shoulders, 'I think your new music is horrible.'

'Ah, it does not appeal to your Hellenic spirit,' replied Crispin carelessly. 'Mephistopheles felt out of place at the classical Walpurgis Night, so you, my dear Caliphronas, feel equally at sea among this diablerie of a Northern composer, so suggestive of the festival on the Bröcken.'

'I don't know what you are talking about,' said the

Count uneasily, having a vague idea he was being laughed at.

'Of course you don't,' replied Crispin coolly. ' You have never read " Faust," neither the first nor the second part.'

Caliphronas knew that Crispin did not like him, and, thinking he wanted to ridicule him in the presence of the ladies, would have made some angry answer, had not Eunice, quite unaware of this storm in a teacup, asked him to sing a Greek song.

'Yes, do, dear Count !' said Mrs. Dengelton gushingly. ' I do so love foreign songs ! They go to the soul.'

'And the soul—at least the English soul—does not understand them,' observed Maurice, with a yawn, for he was growing somewhat tired of this musical discussion.

' If the song is in Italian, French, or German, I can certainly understand it,' said the lady, with dignity ; ' but Greek I can hardly be expected to know.'

'I do 'not think you would care much for the words if you did understand modern Greek,' re-marked Crispin, with a smile. ' The sonorous tongue of Hellas invests the most commonplace poems with a dignity and a charm which they would lose if translated. Come, Count, and sing that love-song you used to be so fond of in Athens.'

'Athens!' repeated the Count, with a significant smile, as he arose to comply with this request.

'Yes, Athens!' repeated Crispin, with emphasis. 'I was accustomed to play your accompaniment. How does it go?'

He began playing a simple melody, which, wild though it was, sounded quite poverty-stricken after the wealth of harmonies which had so distinguished the music of Dvořák. Caliphronas watched the player's fingers for a little time, and then began to sing. He possessed an uncommonly fine tenor voice, though it was somewhat rough for want of training. What he lacked in delicacy, however, he made up in force and fire ; and the wonderful language he sang in also assisted him greatly, though, as regards the song itself neither melody nor words were particularly striking.

Daphne, this summer night is full of singing ;
I hear my comrades sigh at the windows of those they worship ;
The windows are open, but thy lattice is closed.
' Love !' calls the lover to his beloved,
' Love !' answers the beloved with smiling lip.
But from your window you call not ' Love !'
Wherefore the night is empty of singing to me :
Lean from your lattice, capricious one,
And I will sing the strain of the nightingale to the rose.

Yes! you have heard me: you open your window,
I can see the silver daggers gleam in your hair;
And you throw me a rose, which sighs ' I love thee.'
Ah, you have spoken to the rose, and the message is told.
Good-night, my Daphne, sleep with the sound of my voice in
thine ears;
But for me there is no slumber,
For all night will I demand of the rose your message,
And the rose will reply, ' I love thee! I love thee!'

'Thank you so much,' said Eunice, coming over to the piano. 'I do not know what it means, but it sounds wonderfully charming.'

'It is a love-song.'

'I wish I had a translation of it.'

'I will translate it if you wish, Miss Dengelton,' said Crispin, by no means relishing the attention which Eunice was paying to the Greek.

'What! do you know Greek?'

'Modern Greek; yes. I have been in Greece a great deal.'

'A great deal,' echoed Caliphronas, with an evil smile.

Crispin faced round abruptly, and was about to say something in an undertone, but, after a moment's deliberation, turned slowly away. The Count looked after him with a smiling face, and then devoted himself to Eunice, who was by no means averse to receiving his attentions.

Now, Eunice must not be misjudged. It is true that she felt flattered by the attentions of such a strikingly handsome man as Caliphronas; but she was not, as Crispin in his jealousy thought, attracted in any marked degree by this stranger. In fact, she was playing a little comedy for the blinding of her lynx-eyed mother; for, afraid lest that lady should discover that she was secretly engaged to Crispin, with the instinctive craft of womankind, Eunice pretended to be more taken up with the Greek than with the poet. By following this course, she thought her mother's mind would be set at rest concerning the rivalry of Crispin with Maurice. Alas! the plan was a good one, and excellently well carried out ; but such diplomacy met with but an ill reward, as in avoiding Charybdis she fell into the clutches of Scylla; for, in place of an angry mother, she had to put up with an angry lover.

Crispin was puzzled to account for her sudden desertion of him and this marked attention to Caliphronas, so at once, with masculine stupidity, deemed that the outward graces of the Count had rendered her false to him. Had Crispin been fortunate enough to possess a female friend to whom he could have talked on such a serious matter, his suspicions would speedily have been lulled to rest ; for no one but a woman can understand a woman, and Crispin, being of the masculine gender, therefore failed to grasp the situation. Eunice chatted gaily with Caliphronas, smiled on him, sang songs to him, and quite neglected poor Crispin, who towards the end of the night grew almost as melancholy as Maurice, in his despair at such unlooked-for behaviour on the part of the girl he loved.

As to Caliphronas, that gentleman, possessing a considerable amount of vanity, and an overweening sense of his own perfections, saw nothing in the conduct of Miss Dengelton otherwise than what should be. He was so accustomed to be petted and made much of by women, that it became a matter of habit with him, and he would have been considerably astonished had Eunice acted otherwise than she did. At the same time, he was secretly very pleased at making an impression in this quarter, as he saw at once from intercepted glances that the poet was violently enamoured of this fair English maiden. Caliphronas hated Crispin with all the strong venomosity of a little soul, and if he could do him an ill turn would certainly avail himself of the opportunity. Thinking Eunice had succumbed to his fascinations, he was quite prepared to take advantage of his conquest, and deprive the poet of his ewe lamb, the more so as Crispin's ill-concealed jealousy added considerably to the charm of the flirtation. Poor Eunice, who never thought her motives would be misconstrued by her jealous lover, was quite astonished when he permitted Caliphronas to present her with her bedroom candle, and wished her a frosty good-night. She would have liked to have obtained an explanation, but Mrs. Dengelton was at her heels, so she was obliged to retire to bed, considerably disconcerted over the strange behaviour of this stupidly-jealous poet.

Caliphronas also went to bed very shortly, as he did not smoke, and, alleging that it was his custom to retire early and rise early, went off to his room, leaving Crispin alone with Maurice. As soon as they were by themselves, Crispin turned at once to his friend.

'Did you see Eunice to-night?'

Maurice leisurely filled his pipe.

'Yes; I saw her. You are jealous of our friend Caliphronas.'

'Well, I certainly think Eunice gave me good

cause to be so. What is the reason of this sudden change?'

Roylands shrugged his shoulders and lighted his pipe.

'I don't know; unless Francis I. was right,' he said calmly,—'" *Souvent femme varie.*"'

CHAPTER VIII.

ENDYMION.

Oh, goddess wise,
Disdainful of the sultry sun,
Thou waitest till his course is run,
Then stealing where Endymion
In slumber lies,
With am'rous sighs
Awake him in that secret nest,
All drowsy with enchanted rest,
To lie upon thy silver breast :
While daylight dies,
In western skies,
And shyly peering one by one,
The stars gaze on that meeting blest.

FOR the next week or so life passed very agreeably at the Grange, and its inmates, becoming habituated to one another's society, settled down into a lotos-eating existence, which, if not a useful one, was at least infinitely charming. Caliphronas played his part in this country house comedy in the most admirable manner, and, owing to his good looks, his good manners, and his good temper, soon established himself as a universal favourite.

This splendid flower of humanity which had bloomed to such beauty under the serene skies of the East fascinated Maurice greatly, and he took a genuine pleasure in modelling the Endymion from the Count; though at times, in spite of his artistic capabilities, he almost despaired of being able to mould the soft clay into a perfect representation of this virile perfection. At the same time the intercourse between the sculptor and his model was very pleasant, as Caliphronas was a most delightful companion, and told stories of his adventures in a manner worthy of Ulysses or Munchausen.

Yet, though he seemed to grow quite confidential over his past life, he nevertheless withheld many episodes which might have prejudiced his host against him. Maurice, who was simple in many ways, despite his ten years' experience of Bohemia, thought Caliphronas was laying bare his whole soul, whereas the wily Greek only revealed the best side of that very complex article. This setting forth of his moral excellences was of course in keeping with the impression he was anxious to produce, and he thus made himself very agreeable to Maurice, who took the

Count for what he represented himself to be, not for what he really was.

Caliphronas was an excellent conversationalist, and during the sittings beguiled the time with many stories of his countrymen, and not infrequently of his countrywomen, for this Apollo had achieved many conquests in the fields of Venus, and seemed very proud of his prowess during some charming campaigns. Probably most of his stories were exaggerations, and at times even simple Maurice doubted their truth, but so gracefully were these lies told that they sounded as delightful as the tales of Boccaccio. The Count, with considerable imaginative power, supplied to his host a charming history of himself and his early life, which was more or less fictitious ; but, of course, his listener never dreamed that a man could string together such a quantity of consistent lies, and therefore believed those romances worthy of Dumas the Elder. Maurice was no fool, but his own nature was so simple and honourable, that he thought every one else was like himself, and at the worst only deemed that these histories were perhaps highly coloured, but true in the main.

Meanwhile, Eunice had demanded at the most convenient opportunity an explanation from Crispin,

regarding his inexplicable behaviour on that first
night of the Greek's visit, and had received one which
considerably startled her, as it plainly showed that
Crispin was disposed to be jealous. This rather
pleased Eunice, as no woman cares about a meek
lover, and the more jealousy a man displays, the
more his beloved feels complimented at the power
she exercises over his affections. However, the
situation between her and Crispin being somewhat
strained, Eunice, deeming honesty to be the best
policy, confessed all about her little scheme of mis-
leading Mrs. Dengelton regarding the true position of
affairs. On learning the truth, Crispin felt very much
ashamed of his groundless suspicions, and apologised
profusely for having doubted his intended, whereat,
being satisfied with this humbling of the proud, she
took him into favour again, so the course of true love
once more ran smooth.

Notwithstanding the unpleasantness of such a
thing, Crispin rather approved of Eunice treating him
with coldness in the presence of Mrs. Dengelton, as
it would probably lull the suspicions of that lady,
but he was not so sure about his intended accepting
the very pointed attentions of Caliphronas. Crispin
knew the Greek thoroughly. Eunice was absolutely

ignorant of his real character; but as, owing to his being behind the scenes, he could make Caliphronas to a certain extent do what he desired, he hinted very plainly to this Hellenic Don Juan that his attentions were unwelcome to Miss Dengelton, and that he was to give up the *rôle* he had elected to play.

At first the Count was disposed to rebel against this fiat, which put an end to a very pleasant flirtation, but as he really did not care about Eunice, and moreover Crispin was too dangerous to be provoked lightly, he made a virtue of necessity, and ceased to overwhelm the shy English girl with his florid compliments. At the same time he promised himself to be revenged on Crispin at the first opportunity, and Crispin, knowing this, could not help feeling a trifle uneasy, for it was a difficult matter to fight with an absolutely unscrupulous scoundrel like the Count, whose laws were those of neither God nor man, but of his own making. However, Crispin's knowledge of his errand to Roylands proved an effective weapon, and he was satisfied that the Greek would do nothing to jeopardise the success of his mission, even though his vanity demanded some revenge for being thus slighted.

Of course, Mrs. Dengelton still contemplated a match between her daughter and nephew, but

Maurice evaded her hints with great dexterity, yet at the same time, to protect Crispin from a less complaisant rival, made such pointed remarks about the necessity of marriage as led Mrs. Dengelton to believe that he seriously contemplated entering into the matrimonial state.

Never was the good lady so puzzled in her life, for she could not make up her mind as to what Maurice really meant, with his blowing hot one day and cold the next, but, being a great believer in the efficacy of time, deemed it the wisest plan to await the development of events, and in order to watch the same kept her beady eyes wide open. Owing to the neglectful manner in which Eunice had lately treated Crispin, she apprehended no danger from that quarter, and, as Maurice was very attentive to his cousin, the Hon. Mrs. Dengelton felt sure that in the end she would obtain her heart's desire, and install Eunice as mistress of Roylands Grange.

The Rector sometimes came over to the Grange, and was friendly with every one saving Caliphronas, as for some inexplicable reason he professed to heartily dislike that brilliant gentleman. It was certainly a kind of Dr. Fell-ish aversion, of which Mr. Carriston felt rather ashamed, as he could give no plausible reason for such distrust. In reply to a question of Maurice's, he simply said that, much as he admired the physical beauty of the Greek, he was by no means sure that his soul corresponded to the perfection of the body.

Indeed, on one occasion, while Mrs. Dengelton was eulogising the charms of Caliphronas from a feminine point of view, the Rector pointedly quoted that line from the *Odyssey* which says,—' Faultlessly fair bodies are not always the temples of a god-like soul ;' but as this remark was made in Homeric Greek, the significance of it was lost upon the lady. It may be that some subtle instinct warned him against this man, whose evil nature was concealed under the semblance of good ; but at all events the Rector was always on his guard against the Count, and delicately warned Maurice against trusting him too far. Evidently Mr. Carriston had studied the character of Ulysses to no small purpose, and found in Caliphronas a reproduction, body, brain, and soul, of the most crafty of the Greeks.

Regarding the outward appearance of Caliphronas, the Rector was too deeply steeped in the serene literature of Hellas to be unimpressed with the physical splendour of the man. Making allowances for the subduing influence of modern clothing, which

detracts from the most perfect beauty either in man
or woman, Mr. Carriston at times, seeing Caliphronas
in the dazzling sunlight, thought he beheld, as in a
vision, the phantom of some joyous Hellenic divinity
untouched by sorrow or care.

This man, gifted with exceptional beauty, might
have been Hylas, Hyacinth, or Theoxenos, and
strayed by chance from some unknown Arcadian
vale into the rush and turmoil of the modern world,
with its worship of money and position, so alien to
the adoration of Beauty and Genius which formed
the cult of antique Hellas. In truth, Caliphronas
was out of place in England ;—our grey rainy skies,
smoky air, stifling cities, and domesticated Nature,
formed but a dark background for this strongly
vitalised being, tingling from head to foot with the
healthfulness of wild life. He should have dwelt in
the burning south, beside the tideless ripples of serene
seas, under the cloudless blue of Attic skies, with the
silver-grey olives, the shining temples of the gods, and
headland, mountain peak, and island melting into
phantom forms of aerial grace far beyond the expanse
of the laughing ocean. He was an anachronism in
this nineteenth century, the physical survivor of
Hellas as Keats was the mental survivor—one had the

body of Alcibiades, the other the brain of Theocritus,
and both were equally alien to the modern world.

Well was it for the Rector that he could see only
the splendid casket, and not the soul contained
therein, for, in spite of his instinctive distrust, the
fancy he had that this Count was not to be trusted
fell far below the actual moral degradation of the
man. Caliphronas was as vain as a peacock,
absolutely ignorant of the morality of right or wrong,
lazy in every way save what touched his own desires,
and crafty as a fox. Crispin could have pointed out
to the Rector all these flaws, but Crispin had promised to hold his peace so long as Caliphronas
abstained from actual harm; therefore he remained
quiescent, and only reminded the Greek now and
then that there was a watchful eye on his doings.

Maurice believed in the Greek, the Rector doubted
him, and Crispin knew his worthlessness thoroughly,
so among the three of them the character of
Caliphronas was pretty well analysed. From
Maurice the steady respectable Englishman, with his
occasional lapses into artistic wildness, to Caliphronas,
the brilliant cosmopolitan adventurer, was a long step.
Crispin stood midway between the two, as he had a
certain amount of British phlegmatism, with at times

those wild impulses which come from a wandering life and an intellectual nature. Still, he could control his spontaneity, while Caliphronas, obeying his own undisciplined mind, did whatever came into his head ; yet, whenever he scandalised any one by such unconventionality, he would at once obtain forgiveness by the graceful way in which he apologised.

'It is impossible to be angry with you,' said Maurice to him one day, when the Count had been guilty of some ridiculous escapade, 'and yet you deserve to be sharply spoken to. But you are a child in many ways, and we cannot be angry with a child.'

'There you are right, my dear Mr. Maurice,' replied Caliphronas, smiling. 'I am a child, but that is as much as to say, I am a Greek. You remember what the Egyptian priest said to Solon,—"You Greeks are always children." Therefore, if I am a child, and act impulsively like a child, blame my nationality, not myself.'

'I expect you could be a very bad child if you wanted to !' said Crispin, overhearing this defence.

Caliphronas darted a spiteful look at the speaker.

'Very likely,' he replied in a meaning tone ; 'but those who dread stings should not disturb the wasps' nest.'

There was a distinct menace in his tone, but

Crispin felt too confident of having the upper hand to take much notice of this venom, and merely laughed, much to the wrath of the Greek. However, as the time was not yet ripe for action, he restrained his anger, and behaved so amiably to Crispin that it was only the knowledge the poet possessed of his true character that made him mistrust the suave smiles and kindly actions of this Greek Machiavelli.

Caliphronas was an amphibious creature, and lived quite as much in the water as on the shore. Whenever he had the time to spare, he went off to Brasdimir for a dip in the sea, and would plunge and wallow in the water like a dolphin. Fortunately that summer at Roylands was unusually hot, and what with the cloudless skies, the burning sun, and the delicate emerald tints of foliage, grass, and herb, Caliphronas might well have imagined that he was still in his beloved Greece, bathing off some pebbly beach of the Ægean.

Brasdimir was a somewhat peculiar place, and was in reality an arm of the sea (*bras de la mer*) which ran up like a long tongue into the land, where it met the waters of the Roy river. In olden times, Roylands, which was its Norman-French name, had been the property of the crown, and had been used by the Plantagenets for their favourite pastime of hunting.

Henry II. bestowed it on one of his barons who was strongly suspected of being a son of the king, but who on receiving this royal gift dropped his former name of Fitzroy and took that of Roylands. It was certainly a splendid property, and through all the turbulence of succeeding reigns the descendants of the first Roylands had succeeded in keeping their hold on these rich acres; so it was very little diminished in size from the time of its bestowal on Fitzroy. Brasdimir, which was a kind of estuary, ran about half a mile up into the estate, and into it flowed the little river Roy, which was a placid stream of no great beauty. All round Brasdimir lay fat meadows containing some of the finest land in the country, and clumps of beech and elm and oak, remnants of the old hunting-forest of Plantagenet kings, dotted their broad expanse of daisied sward.

Near the upper part of Brasdimir, where it met the waters of the Roy and blended salt with fresh, stood a quincunx of noble oaks which grew close to the bank. From thence the smooth turf of the meadow sloped down to the turbulent waters, and it was here that Caliphronas came to bathe, not only every morning, but often three times a day. Being in the middle of the estate, Brasdimir was far away from

all human habitation, and might have been the navel
of some great wilderness, so lonely it was. The
Greek loved this blending of fresh and salt water, as
the softness of the one assuaged the harshness of the
other, and under the hot sun would frequently cool
himself in this unique pool, which was neither river
nor stream, but a mixture of both.

Very often Crispin and Maurice would come with
him for a morning dip just before sunrise, and then
walk back to the Grange with a tremendous appetite
for breakfast.

One morning they set out for their usual walk, just
as the east was flushing redly with the dawn, and the
chill morning air nipped them keenly as they strolled
along in the direction of Brasdimir. That is to say,
the poet and the sculptor strolled, for Caliphronas
simply danced along, as if to rid himself of his
superabundant energy. Across the dewy meadows
he bounded fawn-like, singing as gaily as the lark
already saluting the sun in the fresh blue sky. Like
some wild being of the woods, he leaped here and there
from very light-heartedness, with his head bare and his
arms tossing in the air. A number of horses pasturing
in the field rushed away at his approach, nor, though he
called them loudly, did they pause in their wild career.

'What a child he is!' said Maurice, watching the graceful figure of the Greek bounding lightly towards the water.

'Yes, a nice child truly,' sneered Crispin, with strong disfavour.

'You don't seem to like Caliphronas?'

'Well, no, I cannot say I do. As an acquaintance he is all very well, but as a friend'— Here Crispin shrugged his shoulders in lieu of words.

'I suppose all he says about himself is true?'

'I suppose so,' replied the poet curtly.

'Do you think he will stay long down here? I hope he will not go away before I finish modelling my Endymion.'

'I think you can safely depend on his staying till then,' rejoined Crispin significantly, and the conversation ended — a conversation which left an odd feeling of discomfort in the mind of Maurice, which —why he could not tell—seemed to revive his old distrust of this fascinating Greek. He would have questioned Crispin further, but as they were now on the edge of the bank, and Caliphronas was within hearing, he had no opportunity of so doing, therefore put off such examination till a more convenient season.

Caliphronas was already in the water, swimming

like a fish, and indeed he was as much at home there
as on the land. The two gentlemen undressed
leisurely on the bank, Maurice making fun of the
Greek as he revelled in his favourite element.

'You had better beware, Caliphronas, as the nymphs
might take a fancy to you as they did to Hylas.'

'River nymphs, sea nymphs, I do not mind in the
least!' cried the Greek gaily; 'ladies are always
charming, whether they have tails or limbs.'

At this moment he reached the opposite bank and
climbed on the fallen trunk of a tree. As he
stood there with his arms raised above his head, the
first yellow ray of the sun flashed on his white body
and enveloped him in glory, as though he were indeed
a stray Olympian. Then, with a shout of glee, he
shot downward like an arrow, cleaving the blue water
with a dash of snowy spray, which sprang upwards
glittering like diamonds in the bright sunlight.
By this time Maurice and his friend were also
enjoying their bathe in the cool element, and the
three rollicked about like schoolboys. Crispin swam
down the estuary in the direction of the sea with
Maurice, and soon the surface of the water roughened
by the wind began to dash salt spray in their faces.
Caliphronas stayed where he was, amusing himself

with fancy strokes, but after a time he became tired, and when the others came back, breathless with their long swim, they found the Count standing on the bank drying himself.

As they also were tired, they also sought the bank, but at this moment one of the horses, a powerful black one, came timidly near them. Caliphronas, with that wonderful power he had over all animals, advanced, nude as he was, up the bank, and called to the horse in a coaxing tone. The animal let him get quite close to it and lay his hand on the mane, when with a sudden spring the Greek leaped on its back, and the horse, startled by the action and by his shout, galloped away at full speed. Round and round the meadow went horse and man, forming so striking a sight that Maurice and Crispin paused in their dressing to look at it. As the horse at full gallop came sweeping past, with Caliphronas laughing and holding on by the mane, Maurice involuntarily thought of the frieze of the Parthenon, where nude youths ride fiery steeds in a long serene procession of marble figures. The Greek rode like a Red Indian, with the most consummate ease, and as the horse for the third time darted past the quincunx of oaks, he dropped lightly off, by some trick known only to himself, and the steed galloped wildly away, while the Greek came back laughing to his friends.

'What a child you are, Caliphronas!' said Maurice in a vexed tone; 'riding a bare-backed steed in that reckless manner. You might have broken your neck.'

'Small loss if he had,' muttered Crispin under his breath.

'Oh, I can stick on anything,' answered Caliphronas carelessly, taking no notice of Crispin's remark, which his keen ears immediately heard; 'besides, that gallop has done me good. See, I am quite dry.'

When they were dressed, the three of them walked quickly back to breakfast, for the morning air had developed their appetites enormously. Mrs. Dengelton and Eunice awaited them on the terrace, and they were soon seated round the well-spread table. Caliphronas, touching neither coffee nor tea, drank water only, and confined his eating to bread, honey, and eggs. His were the tastes of primeval man, and he strongly disliked the elaborate dishes which were so pleasing to the cultured palates of his more civilised neighbours.

'I do not know how you can eat such things,' he said in some disgust, as Eunice took some curry. 'Does it not make you ill?'

'Not in the least, Count,' she replied, laughing. 'It is a very depraved taste, I suppose, but I am very fond of curry.'

'And tea—hot tea,' retorted Caliphronas quickly. 'I have heard it said that tea is bad for the nerves. Ladies always complain of nerves, yet they drink tea.'

'I could not do without my tea,' said Mrs. Dengleton, who was given to surreptitious cups of tea at odd hours of the day, 'and yet I have nerves. Oh, those dreadful nerves! You don't know what it is to be so afflicted, Count.'

'No, I do not. I never had an illness in my life, but then that is because I live a natural life, whereas all you highly-civilised people live an artificial existence. If you gave up your highly-spiced dishes, your strong wines, your late hours, your breathing of poisonous air, you would be as healthy as I am.'

'Well, you can hardly call the air of Roylands poisonous,' said Maurice indolently.

'No, the air here is delightful because you live near the sea. I could not dwell inland myself. I should die. I must breathe the sea air, see the wide waste of waters, hear the thunder of waves on the beach. That is the only life for a healthy man.'

'You could not live in London, I suppose,' said Mrs. Dengelton, frowning on Eunice, who was talking in a quiet tone to Crispin.

'London!' cried the Count, with scorn. 'I would as soon live at the bottom of the sea. Indeed, I believe it would be healthier there. London, that crushed-up mass of houses inhabited by pale-faced people—I wonder they can exist. Oh, I saw and heard a good deal of London when I was there. Your people in the East End never leave those narrow streets from one year to the other. They know nothing of sunrise or sunset, for they only see those marvels through a smoky veil. They cannot tell a bird by its song—they know nothing of animals or their habits. Of the wonderful life of Nature which is born and lives and dies in the woods, in the seas, in the mountains, they are ignorant. They are born blind, they live blind, they die blind, and call such blindness, life.'

'But what about the people in the West End?' asked Mrs. Dengelton, with the air of making a crushing remark.

'They are scarcely better,' retorted Caliphronas promptly; 'they sit half the night in theatres breathing hot air, they go to balls where there is such a crowd of people that no one can dance, they walk for an hour in the Park and call it exercise, they poison themselves at the clubs with cigarettes, and in the boudoirs with tea—and all this feverish, unreal life is called "the season." When they go abroad it is to Monte Carlo and those sort of places, where they lead the same life on a smaller scale. No, the West End is no better than the East End!'

'But you forget,' said Crispin, more from a desire to contradict the Count than because he disagreed with him, 'plenty of people go mountaineering, game-shooting, yachting, exploring.'

'I know all that, my dear friend, but the number of people who do those things is very small. I am talking of the great mass of the English people, and so far as I can see, whether they are rich or poor, the life they lead is in both cases equally opposed to health and enjoyment.'

'Here endeth the first reading,' said Maurice, rising from the table, his example being followed by all his guests. 'Caliphronas, you are quite eloquent on the subject.'

'Yes! I am not usually so eloquent,' replied the Count, going out on to the terrace, 'but on all sides I hear from your people complaints of being ill.

Well, the remedy is in their own hands.   Why don't they use it ? '

'My good sir,' remarked Crispin, who had lighted a cigarette, 'you cannot overturn the whole complex civilisation of the West in that manner.   Man can no more go back to the simplicity of the existence you eulogise, than you could settle down to a fashionable life in London and enjoy it.'

'Well, you at least can be cured easily,' said the Count, with emphasis, for, as they were now beyond earshot of the rest of the party, he could talk freely ; 'you all your life have lived the life of a natural man, but now you smoke that horrible tobacco, drink all kinds of wines, eat all kinds of dishes, and will soon become as artificial as those people around you.'

'Perhaps I shall come back to the primeval existence you praise.'

'With that young lady, I suppose ? '

'Perhaps.'

'Ah, she is very charming !   She is '—

'Thank you, I don't want to hear your opinion of Miss Dengelton,' said Crispin haughtily ; 'your primeval simplicity at times verges on rudeness. How long are you going to stay here ? '

' I can't tell you that; but I am going to take my first step to-day.'

' In order to get Roylands to Melnos?'

' Yes. Oh, I have a lure, my friend. Yes; I have described the fairyland of the islands, and that it is fairyland you must admit. He is even now seized with a desire of going there, so to-day I will get him to make up his mind to go with me to the Levant.'

' How?'

' I will show him this.'

Crispin looked at the portrait the Count held out, which was that of a marvellously beautiful woman in a Greek dress.

' Helena!' cried the poet, recognising the face. ' When did she get this taken? Has she been to Athens?'

' No. I took it myself. Oh, I am not absolutely the barbarian you think me. I have gone in for photography. Yes; this is one of my best efforts.'

' And do you think that face will lure Maurice to the East?'

' It ought to,' said Caliphronas, gazing at the picture with a burning light in his eyes; 'she is as lovely as her namesake of Troy, and I love her, oh, how I love her!'

'Is it wise, do you think, to introduce a possible rival?'

'That does not matter to me,' replied the Count, slipping the picture into his pocket. 'I have Justinian's promise.'

'Yes, but you have not got Helena's.'

'Oh, she won't refuse to marry me.'

'For the sake of her happiness, I hope she will.'

'You are very complimentary,' retorted the Greek ironically, turning away. 'Well, I must leave your delightful society, my friend. It is time for me to go to the studio.'

'Wait a minute! I have not thwarted your plans, because, so far as I can see, they are innocent, but if you induce Maurice to go to the Levant'—

'Well?' demanded Caliphronas insolently.

'I shall go also.'

'And your reason?'

'A very simple one. I do not trust the scamp called Andros.'

'Better known, at least in England, as Constantine Caliphronas,' replied the Count coolly. 'Well, come if you like, to watch over your precious friend. I do not wish him harm, but he, and you also, had better beware of Justinian.'

CHAPTER IX.

THE PORTRAIT.

Dreary life,
Aching fears,
Endless strife,
Bitter tears,
Lo, a lovely face I see,
Changing all the world to me.

Love's delight,
Beauty's face,
Smilings bright,
Woman's grace,
These beholding all in thee,
Thou hast changed the world to me.

THE studio which Maurice had fitted up for himself at the Grange was a very work-manlike apartment, being quite barren of the artistic frippery with which painters love to decorate their rooms. Sculpture is a much more virile art than painting, and, scorning frivolous adorn-ments of all kinds, the artist of the chisel devotes

himself to the severest and highest forms of beauty,
so that he finds quite enough loveliness in his coldly
perfect marble figures, without furnishing his studio
like a Wardour Street toy-shop.   Of course, he who
works in colours loves to gaze on colours; and therefore
a fantastic Eastern carpet, a quaint figured tapestry, a
gold-broidered curtain of Indian silk, a yellow shield
of antique workmanship, a porous red jar from Egypt,
and such like brilliances, are pleasing to the artistic
eye, and the constant sight of their blended hues
keep the sense of colour, so to speak, up to the mark.
The sculptor, however, has but one colour, white, which
is not a colour; and the less luxurious his studio, the
more likely is he to concentrate his attention on the
statue growing to perfection under his busy chisel.

These sentiments, which would seem to narrow
down a sculptor to the severest and least graceful
form of art, were uttered by Crispin in approval of
that bare barn attached to the Grange which Maurice
called his studio.   But then Crispin knew nothing
about art, and a painter or a sculptor reading the
above views of their profession will probably laugh
to scorn such fanciful notions.   Yet it is true that
the sculptor by his art is shut off from the world of
colour, unless, like the old Greeks,—according to some

critics,—he tints his statues, and thereby turns them into wax figures. But doubtless those Hellenic sculptors who wrought nude gods and draped goddesses from the marbles of Paros and Pentelicus, did not fail to notice how the background of the blue Attic sky enhanced the beauty of their creations, and therefore must have concluded that the world of colour, to which they were strangers, could accentuate the fairness and beauty of their statues. Again, these are the artistic sentiments of Crispin the poet, delivered to Maurice with much daring, seeing the speaker was ignorant of the world of art, and only promulgated his ideas in a purely poetical fashion. But Crispin's crude view of art and artists may doubtless fail to interest many people ; therefore, to come back in a circle to the starting-point of the disquisition, Maurice's studio was a very workmanlike apartment.

The floor consisted merely of bare boards, although at one end, in front of the fireplace, there was an oasis of carpet, on which rested a table for pipes and tobacco, together with two comfortable arm-chairs. Scattered here and there were statues finished and unfinished, some completed in marble, others incomplete in clay. Maurice had gratified his artistic desires for the perfection of sculpture by surrounding himself with

copies in marble of some famous statues, for now, as
he was wealthy, he could afford to do so. Here danced
the Faun with his grotesque visage and lissome pose ;
there smiled Hebe, holding her cup for the banqueting
of the gods ; Bacchus with his crown of vine-leaves
gazed serenely on the sad face of the draped Ariadne
in the distance ; Apollo watched the lizard crawling up
the tree-trunk ; and Hermes, with winged feet, poised
himself on his pedestal as if for flight. The whole
studio was filled with the fair and gracious forms of
Greek art, and no wonder at times Maurice despaired
of producing anything worth looking at beside these
immortal productions of the Hellenic brain and hands.

The great necessity now is, not to know what
one can do, but what one cannot do ; and if many
of our complacent artists, poets, sculptors, novelists,
only abided by this rule, the world would be spared
the perpetration of many an atrocity in marble, verse,
or on canvas, which the conceited creators think
perfection. Maurice Roylands had a pretty taste for
chipping marble, but he was by no means a genius,
and his statues, while perfectly wrought in accordance
with the canons of art, yet lacked that soul which
only the true sculptor can give to his creations. It
was a fortunate thing for him that he was a rich man,

for assuredly he would never have become a great
sculptor. His ideas were excellent, but he could not
carry them out in accordance with the figment of his
brain, as he lacked the divine spark of genius which
alone can fully accomplish that which it conceives.

At present, clad in a blouse, he was standing in
front of a mass of wet clay, manipulating the soft
material with dexterous fingers into a semblance of
the fanciful Endymion of his brain and the real
Endymion of Caliphronas. That gentleman was
posed on the model's platform in the distance, and
was beguiling the time by incessant chattering of this,
that, and the other thing.

The artist had based his conception of this statue
of Endymion on these lines of Keats, poet laureate to
Dian herself,—

> *What is there in the Moon that thou shouldst move*
> *My heart so potently?*

He intended to represent the shepherd sitting on
Latmos top, chin on hand, gazing at the moon with
dreamy eyes, his mortal heart thrilling at the thought
that he would see the inviolate Artemis incarnate in
the flesh. In accordance with the Greek ideas of
nudity, Maurice did not drape his statue ; but the
shepherd sat on his chlamys, which was lightly

thrown over a rock, while beside him lay scrip, and flask, and pastoral crook. Caliphronas was seated thus,—his elbow resting on his knee and his chin on his hand, gazing presumably at the moon, in reality at Maurice, while the other hand lightly hung down by his side, and his left leg was drawn back so that the foot bent in a delicate curve was calculated to show its full beauty. This pose showed all the perfect lines of his figure, and with his nude body, his clean-shaven face, and dreaming eyes, he looked the veritable Endymion who was awaiting the descent of the goddess from high Olympus. Though it was a warm day, a fire burned in the grate, for the Greek was very susceptible to cold, and after working for some time Maurice was fain to rest, so great was the heat ; whereupon Caliphronas flung himself back on the chlamys, placed his hands behind his head, and began to talk.

'Shall you be long at your work to-day, Mr. Maurice?' he asked with a yawn.

'No, not if you are tired,' replied Roylands, throwing a cloak over the Count. 'You had better wrap yourself up, or you will catch cold. If you don't care to sit any more to-day, we can leave off now.'

'Well, I have some letters to write, but I will wait another half-hour.'

'All right!'

Maurice lighted his favourite pipe and established himself in a comfortable chair, upon which the Count, finding the rock of Endymion somewhat hard, forsook the platform, and, wrapping the cloak closely round him, sat down opposite the sculptor.

'I wonder you don't smoke, Caliphronas,' said Maurice, idly watching the Greek with half-closed eyes. 'You would find it an excellent way of passing the time.'

'Of killing time, I suppose you mean ; but I have no need to do that. At least, not when I am at home in Greece. Here, yes, it is rather difficult to get through the day comfortably ; if it were not for these sittings, I really do not know what I should do with myself.'

'I am afraid I shall never be able to carry out my conception of Endymion,' said Maurice, paying no attention to this remark.

Caliphronas shrugged his shoulders.

'Oh, your work is very good,' he said politely, 'very good indeed ; but of course it is not perfect.'

'I know that, but practice makes perfect.'

'Not in the world of art. You may learn to paint in strict accordance with the rules of art. You may sculpture to the inch every portion of the human body, but that is only the outward semblance of the picture or the statue. The essential thing which makes a work great is the soul.'

'Quite true. And you think I cannot create the soul of my statues?' said Maurice, rather nettled at the outspoken criticism.

'I say nothing, my friend. I know but little of art, so it would be an impertinence of me to talk about that of which I am ignorant.'

'The longer we live the less do we find we know,' said Roylands sententiously.

'I suppose that is true,' replied Caliphronas indolently; 'but, thank Heaven, I have not the soul of an artist, for it seems to cause its owner perpetual anxiety. No; I live a life healthy, joyous, and free, like the other animals of Nature, and I am quite satisfied.'

'Is that not rather ignoble?'

'Perhaps; but that is nothing to me. I am happy, which is, to my mind, the main aim of life. Why should I slave for money? I do not wish it. Why should I toil for years at art, and gain at the end but ephemeral fame? Besides, when one dies, what good does fame do? A large marble tomb would not please me.'

'Still, the fame of being spoken of by succeeding generations.'

'Who would do nothing but wrangle over their different opinions regarding one's work. Present happiness is what I wish, not future praise; but in this narrow island of yours you cannot understand the joy of life. Come with me to the isles of Greece, and you will be so fascinated with the free, wild life that you will never return to your prison-house.'

'If all men thought like you, the world would not progress.'

'I don't want all men to think the same as I do,' replied the Count selfishly. 'I suppose there must be slaves as well as freemen. I prefer to be the last.'

'Slaves!'

'Yes. I do not mean the genuine article, but all men are slaves more or less, if they don't follow my mode of life. Slaves to gain, slaves to art, slaves to conventionality, slaves to everything; and what do they gain by such slavery? Nothing but what I do —a tomb—annihilation.'

'Well, you are a slave to your passions.'

'You mean I obey my impulses. Well, I do; but it is a very pleasant kind of slavery.'

'And you believe in that horrible theory of annihilation?'

'Well, I don't know in what I believe. I trouble

myself in nowise about the hereafter. I am alive, I am strong, I am happy. The sun is bright, the winds are inspiriting,—I draw delight from mountain and plain,—so why should I trouble myself about that of which I know nothing? The present is just enough for me. Let the future take care of itself.'

'A selfish philosophy.'

'A very enjoyable one. Come with me to the East, and you will adopt my creed. Are you happy here?'

'No.'

'I can see that. You are melancholy at times, you are devoured with spleen, you find the life you lead too dreary for your soul. If you let me be your physician, I will cure you.'

'And how?'

'By a very simple means. I will make you lead the same life as I do myself,—open-air life,—and in a few months you will find these nightmares of the soul completely disappear. No prisoner can be happy; and you, a prisoner in this dungeon of convention-ality, swathed in the mummy cloths of civilisation, cannot hope to be happy unless you go out into the wilderness.'

'The life you describe is purely an animal one. What about the intellect?'

'Intellect! pshaw! I know more about Nature than half your scientific idiots with their books.'

'What an inconsistent being you are, Caliphronas!' said Maurice in an amused tone. 'You say you love art, admire pictures, adore statues; yet, if every man followed the life you eulogise, such things would not be in existence.'

'I tell you, I don't want all the world to follow my example. I should be very sorry to lose all these delights of the senses, so I am glad there are men sufficiently self-denying to slave at such things for my delight; but, as regards myself, I desire to live as a natural man—an animal, as you say. It is ignoble—yes; but it is pleasant.'

This speech somewhat opened the eyes of Maurice to the kind of soul which was enshrined in the splendid body of this man; and he saw plainly that the sensual part of Caliphronas had completely conquered the spiritual. But with what result?—that this ignoble being was happy. What an ironical comment of Fate on the strivings of great beings to subordinate the senses to the soul. The soul agitated by a thousand fears, the brain striving ever after the impossible—what do these give their possessor, but a feeling of unrest, of unsatisfied hunger; whereas the body, untortured by an inquiring spirit, brought contentment, happiness—ignoble though they were—to the animal man.

By this time, Caliphronas, having made up his mind to sit no more that day, was slowly dressing himself, singing a Greek song in his usual gay manner.

> ' *Three girls crossed my path in the twilight;*
> *One did I love, but the others were nothing to me :*
> *She frowned at my greeting, but her friends smiled sweetly,*
> *Yet was she the loveliest of them all,*
> *And I loved her frown more than their smiles inviting.*'

' How happy you are, Caliphronas ! '

' Thoroughly.   I have not a care in the world. Come with me to the Island of Fantasy, and you also will be happy.'

' The Island of Fantasy ! '

' Yes ; that is what Justinian calls it.'

' Who is Justinian ? — anything to do with the Pandects ? '

' Pandects ? ' reiterated Caliphronas, puzzled by the word.

' Yes.   Is he a ruler—a law-giver ? '

' Oh yes ; he is the king of the Island of Fantasy.'

' Which, I presume, exists only in your brain,' said Roylands jestingly.

' Pardon me, no,' replied the Count seriously,

resuming his seat. 'The Island of Fantasy, or, to call it by its real name, Melnos, does exist in the Ægean Sea. It is an island but little known, and Justinian, who is my very good friend, rules over it as a kind of Homeric king. Ulysses was just such another; and there you will find the calm, patriarchal life of those bygone times, which you of the modern world think has vanished for ever. My friend, the Golden Age still exists in Melnos, and if you come with me, you will dwell in Arcady.'

'My dear Count,' said Maurice, much impressed by the ease of the man's speech, 'I have never yet heard a foreigner speak our tongue so felicitously as you do. Where did you attain such fluency—such a good accent?'

'Ah, I will tell you that when we arrive at Melnos.'

'You are almost as much of a riddle as is Crispin,' said Maurice, chafing at this secrecy, which seemed to be so senseless.

'Doubtless; but if you are curious to know about us both, come to the Ægean with me.'

'About you both?' repeated the Englishman; 'why, do you know anything of Crispin?'

Caliphronas knew a good deal about Crispin, but he was too wise to say so. Silence regarding the past on his part, was the only way to secure silence on the part of Crispin ; and much as Caliphronas, in his enmity to the poet, would have liked to reveal what Crispin desired to be kept secret, he had too much at stake to risk such a gratification of his spite, and therefore passed off the question with a laugh.

'Know anything about Crispin?' he reiterated, smiling. 'I am afraid I know no more than you do. I met him at Athens, truly, but we were but acquaintances, so I never made any inquiries about him. He was as much a riddle there as here. Oh yes, I heard all the romances about him in London ; and no doubt one story is as true as another. The reason I made such a remark as I did, was that, as Crispin says himself, he came from the East like a wise man of to-day ; you will probably learn his past history in those parts.'

'And as to yourself?'

'Eh! I have told you all my past life, with the exception of that portion of it which I spent in Melnos, and that I did not think worth while relating. But it is a charming place, I assure you ; and if you come with me, I am confident you will find a community under the rule of Justinian, which is quite foreign to this century.'

'I have a great mind to accept your offer,' said Maurice musingly; 'there is nothing to keep me in England, and a glimpse of new lands would do me good. Besides, Count, one does not get such an excellent guide as you every day.'

'Oh, I know every island in the Ægean,' replied Caliphronas, smiling his thanks for the compliment. 'I have sailed all over the Archipelago, and am quite a sailor in a small way. Lesbos, Cythera, Samos, Rhodes,—I know them all intimately; so if you are fond of ruins, and the remains of old Greece, I can show you plenty, tell you the legends, arrange about the inns, and, in fact, act as a dragoman; but, of course, without his greed for money.'

' It seems worth considering.'

'It will be a visit to paradise,' cried Caliphronas enthusiastically, springing to his feet. 'Here you do not know the true meaning of the word beauty. Only under the blue sky, above the blue waves of the Ægean, is it to be seen. Aphrodite arose from those waters, and she was but an incarnation of the beauty which meets the eye on all sides. You have been my host in England. I will be your host in Greece, and will entertain you in my ruined abode,— misnamed a palace,—which is all that remains to me

of my forefathers.   Together we will sail over those
laughing waters, and see the sun-kissed islands bloom
on the wave.   Paradise!   It is the Elysian fields of
foam where rest the spirits of wearied mariners.
What says the song of the Greek sailors?

> *'I will die! but the earth will not hold me in her breast,*
> *For the blue sea will clasp me in its arms.*
> *I will die! but let my soul not find the heaven of the orthodox.*
> *Nay, let it wander among the flowery islands,*
> *Where I can see my home and the girl who mourns me.*
> *That only is the paradise I long for.'*

'You forget I do not know modern Greek,' said
Maurice, smiling at the enthusiasm of the Count ;
'nor indeed much ancient Greek, for the matter of
that.   But see, Count, you have dropped a photograph.'

'You can look at it,' said the Count, who had let it
fall purposely ; 'I have no secrets.'

'Oh!'

'Ah, you think it a charming face?'

'Charming is too weak a word.   It is Aphrodite
herself.'

'Alas!' cried Caliphronas, with a merry laugh ;
'that goddess lived before the days of sun-pictures,
else Apollo might have photographed her.   No ;
that is no deity, but a mortal maiden whom I saw

at Melnos. It is not bad for an amateur effort, is it ? '

' Oh, very good, very good ! ' replied Maurice hurriedly ; ' but the face—what a heavenly face ! '

' Ah, you see my paradise has got its Eve.'

' And its Adam, doubtless ? '

' No, there is no Adam to that Eve,' said Caliphronas, shaking his head ; ' at least, there was not when I was in Melnos six months ago. Why should there be ? You will find plenty of women as beautiful as Helena.'

' Helena—is that her name ? Yes, I have no doubt you will find beautiful women in Greece,—'tis their heritage from Phryne, Lais, and Aspasia ; but none can be so beautiful as Helen of Troy.'

' Possibly not; but that woman is Helena of Melnos, not of Troy.'

' I'll swear she is as beautiful as the wife of Menelaus, whom Paris loved.'

' You seem quite in raptures over this face,' said Caliphronas, with but ill-concealed anger. ' Pray, do you propose to be Menelaus or Paris ? '

' Why, are you in love with her yourself ? ' asked Maurice, looking at the Greek in some surprise.

This question touched Caliphronas more nearly

than Maurice guessed, but, whatever passion he may have felt for the lady of the picture, he said nothing about it, but laughed in a somewhat artificial manner.

' I in love with her, my friend ?　No ; she is beautiful, I grant you, but I look upon her as I would upon an exquisite picture.　She is nothing to me.　Did I not tell you I have a future bride in the East?　Yes —in Constantinople ; a daughter of the old Byzantine nobles, a Fanariot beautiful as the dawn, who dwells at Phanar.'

' Then I need fear no rivalry from you, Caliphronas ? '

' Certainly not.　But you seem to have fallen in love with this pictured Helena.'

' I will not go so far as to say that ; but you know I have the artistic temperament, and therefore admire beauty always.'

' Of course — the artistic sense,' sneered Caliphronas in such a disagreeable way, that Maurice again looked at him in astonishment.

The fact is, that Roylands' admiration of the portrait seemed to ruffle Caliphronas very much, and quite altered his usual nonchalance of manner.　Never before had Maurice seen his joyous nature so changed, for he had now a frown on his usually smiling face, and appeared to be on the verge of an angry outbreak. All the wild beast in his nature, which was so carefully hidden by the civilised mask, was revealed in the most unexpected manner, and with flashing eyes, tightly drawn lips, and scowling countenance, he looked anything but the serene Greek with whom Roylands was acquainted. Maurice was astonished and rather annoyed at this exhibition of temper, so, rising from his seat, he gave the picture back to his guest with a dignified gesture.

'I have no wish to pry into your secrets, Count,' he said quietly, walking towards the door; 'you showed me that portrait of your own free will, and if I admire it somewhat warmly, surely the beauty of the face is my excuse. At present I will say *au revoir*, as I have some business to do, and shall be in my study till luncheon.'

When Maurice disappeared, the Greek stamped about the room in sheer vexation at having betrayed himself, for he could not but see, that for once this simple Englishman had caught a glimpse of his real nature, hitherto so carefully concealed.

'I am a fool, a fool!' he said savagely in Greek; 'everything was going well, and I spoil all by letting my temper get the better of me. Why did I not let him admire Helena and say nothing? When we get to Melnos, that will be a different thing, for Justinian cannot go back from his word; and if I perform my part of the bargain, and bring this fool to Melnos, he must perform his, and give me his daughter. I must recover my lost ground if possible, —bah! it will not be difficult. I can see he is in love with Helena, so that will smooth everything. In love with my goddess!' he said ardently, gazing at the lovely face. 'Ah, how can he help being so?—there is much excuse; but he can only worship you at a distance, my Venus, for you are mine—mine—mine!'

He thrust the picture into his pocket, and, recovering his serene joyousness of mood, pondered for a few moments as to what was the best course to pursue. At last he decided, and walked towards the door of the studio with the air of a man who had made up his mind.

'I will give him the picture,' he said, with a great effort, 'and I feel sure he will make peace on those terms.'

Maurice was sitting at his desk, wondering why the even-tempered Greek had thus given way to anger over the picture.

'If he is engaged to a lady of Stamboul, he cannot

be in love with this Helena,' he said to himself.
'Perhaps he was jealous of my admiring the beauty
of a woman more than his own. All Greeks are
vain, but, so far as I can see, Caliphronas is simply
mad with vanity. Come in.'

In answer to his invitation, the Count entered
smiling, and laid the picture on the desk before
Maurice.

'You must not be angry with me, my friend,' he
said volubly; 'I am like a child, and grow bad-
tempered over nothing. This Helena is nothing to
me, and, to prove this, I give you her portrait, which
I do not care to keep. Come, am I forgiven?'

'Of course you are,' said Roylands hastily; 'but
I will not deprive you of your picture.'

'No, no, I do not want it back,' replied Caliphronas, spreading out his hands in token of refusal;
'you love the face, so keep it by all means.'

'She is very beautiful,' said Maurice, gazing long-
ingly at this modern Helen.

'Is she worth a journey to the East?' asked Caliphronas in a soft voice, like the sibilant hiss of a
serpent.

Maurice made no reply; he was looking at the
portrait.

CHAPTER X.

A MODERN IXION.

Oh, beware
Of a snare!
'Tis a phantom fair
Who will tangle your heart in her golden hair.

Tho' he vowed
Would be bowed
Heaven's Hera proud,
Ixion was duped by a treacherous cloud.

But in sooth,
Fate hath ruth,
And this dream of youth
May change from a dream to immutable truth.

HAT is truth?' asked Pilate, but to this perplexing question he received no answer, not even from the Divine Man, who was best able to give a satisfactory reply. In the same way we may ask, 'What is love?' and receive many answers, not one of which will be correct. The reason being that no one knows what love is, though every one has felt it. The commonest things are generally the most perplexing, and surely love is common enough, seeing it is the thing upon which the welfare, the pleasure, nay, the continuity, of the human race depends. Yet no one can define this everyday passion, because it is undefinable. ''Tis the mutual feeling which draws man and maid together.' True; but that may be affection, which is a lesser passion than love. ''Tis the admiration of a man or a woman for each other's beauty.' Nay, that is but sensuality. ''Tis the longing of two people of the opposite sexes to dwell together all their life.' Why, that is only companionship. Affection, sensuality, companionship, all three very pleasant, very comforting, but Love is greater than such a trinity. He may not give pleasure, he may not bring comfort, on the contrary, he may make those to whose hearts he comes very unhappy. Love is no mischievous urchin, who plays with his arrows; no, he is a great and terrible divinity, who comes to every mortal but once in life. We desire him, we name him, we delight in him; but we know not what he is, where he comes from, or when he will leave us.

These reflections were suggested to Maurice by

the extraordinary feelings with which this dream-
face of Helena had inspired him. Never before
had he felt the sensation of love,—not affection, not
admiration, but strong, passionate love, which pervaded his whole being, yet which he could not
describe. He had not seen this woman in the flesh,
he was hardly certain if she existed, for the only
evidences he had to assure him that there was such
a being were the portrait and the name, yet he felt,
by some subtle, indescribable instinct, that this was
the one woman in the world for him. Maurice, who
had hitherto doubted the existence of love, was now
being punished for such scepticism, and was as love-
sick as ever was some green lad fascinated by a
pretty face. 'He jests at scars who never felt a
wound;' but Maurice did not jest at scars now,
for the arrow of Cupid, shot from some viewless
height, had made a wound in his heart which would
heal not till he died; or, even granting it would
heal, would leave a scar to be seen of all men.

It was the old story of Ixion over again. Here
was a man embracing a cloudy phantom of his own
imagination, for, admitting that this beautiful face
belonged to a real woman, Maurice knew nothing
about her, yet dowered her with all the exquisite

perfections of feminality. He dreamed she would
be loving, tender, and womanly, yet, for aught he
knew, the owner of that lovely face might be a very
Penthesilea for daring and masculine emulation.
But no; he could not believe that she would unsex
herself by taking upon her nature the rival attributes
of manly strength, for the whole face breathed
nothing but feminine delicacy. That broad white
brow, above which the hair was smoothed in the
antique fashion ; those grave, earnest eyes, so full of
sympathy and purity ; that beautifully shaped mouth,
like a scarlet flower, speaking of reticence and
womanly shrinking. No; he was quite sure that
she was an ideal woman, therefore worshipped her
—unseen, unheard—with all the chivalrous affection
of a mediæval knight.

Day and night that faultless face haunted his brain
like some perfect poem, and, waking or sleeping, he
seemed to hear her voice, full and rich as an organ-
note, calling on him to seek her in that Island of
Fantasy whereof the Greek had spoken. Was she
indeed some fairy princess, detained in an enchanted
castle against her will? was this mysterious Justinian,
whose personality seemed so vague, indeed her jailor,
guarding her as the dragon did the golden fruit of

the Hesperides? and was Caliphronas a messenger
sent to tell him of the reward awaiting him should
he take upon him vows to release her from such
thraldom, and accomplish his quest successfully?
Curious how the classic legends and the mediæval
romances mixed together in his brain, yet one and
all, however diverse in thought, pointed ever to that
beautiful woman dwelling in an enchanted island en-
circled by the murmurous waves of the blue Ægean.

True, he had fallen in love, and thus regained in
one instant the interest in life which he had lost
erstwhile; but the object of his adoration seemed
so far away, her personality, about which he could
only obscurely conjecture, was so lost in dream-
mists, that the cure for his melancholia seemed worse
than the disease itself. He again became sad and
absent-minded, grieving — not, as formerly, for a
vague abstraction, a something, he knew not what
—but for an actual being, for an unfulfilled passion
which seemed in itself as elusive a thing as had
tormented him formerly. The indistinct phantom
which had engendered melancholia had taken shape
—the shape of a beautiful, smiling face, which
mocked him with the promise of delight probably
never destined to be fulfilled.

All his guests noticed this lapse into his former melancholy, but none of them guessed the reason save Caliphronas, who was beside himself with rage at the discovery. The stratagem with which he proposed to draw Maurice to Melnos had succeeded beyond his highest expectations, but he was very dissatisfied with his success, and began to wonder if Crispin was not right after all concerning the folly of presenting a possible rival to the woman he desired for himself. The woman was to be the reward of his success; he had made use of that woman's pictured loveliness to achieve that success, and by so doing had complicated the simplicity of the affair by introducing a third element, that of a rival's love, which might place an obstacle in the way of his receiving the reward.

It was Mephistopheles showing Faust the phantom of Gretchen, and the same result of love for an unseen woman had ensued; but then, Mephistopheles was not enamoured of the loveliness he used as a bait to catch his victim, whereas Caliphronas was. However, it was too late now to alter the matter, for the Greek could see that Maurice had almost made up his mind to go in search of this new Helen of Troy, and if he succeeded in gaining her heart, circumstances might arise with which it would be difficult to grapple.

After all, when Caliphronas compared the English-man's everyday comeliness with his own glorious beauty, he felt that no woman would refuse him for such a commonplace individual as his possible rival. But, again, Caliphronas was aware that Helena valued the inward more than the outward man, in which case he suspected he had but little chance in coming off best. Pose as he might to the world, Caliphronas knew the degradation of his own soul, and when this was contrasted with the honest, proud, straightforward nature of Maurice Roylands, it could be easily seen which of them the woman would choose as best calculated to ensure her happiness. Besides, the love which had been newly born in Maurice's heart was a highly spiritual passion, with no touch of grossness, whereas the desires of Caliphronas were purely animal ones for physical beauty. In point of outward semblance, he would have been a fitter husband for the exquisite beauty of this woman, but as to a marriage of souls, which after all is the only true marriage, the one was as different from the other as is day from night.

Maurice said nothing to Crispin about the portrait, and though the latter guessed from his abstraction that Caliphronas had played his last card with that hidden loveliness, he made no remark, for the time was not yet ripe to unfold the past. If, however, Maurice went to Melnos, Crispin, as he had told Caliphronas, determined to accompany him, as much on his own account as on that of his friend.

Truly this poet was a riddle, as was also the Greek; but it is questionable if Maurice, with his open and above-board English life, was not a greater riddle than either of these mysterious men, seeing that his perplexity was a thing of the soul, vague and intangible, the solution of which meant the settling of his whole spiritual life; whereas the lighting of the darkness with which Caliphronas and Crispin chose to enshroud themselves was simply a question of material existence.

The Parcæ held the three tangled skeins in their hands: Clotho now grasped the intricate threads; Lachesis was spinning the actions which were to lead to the unravelling of these riddles of spiritual and material things; and Atropos was waiting grimly with her fatal scissors to clip the life-thread of one of the three. But the question was, which? Ah, that was yet to be seen! for the middle Destiny was yet weaving woof and warp of words, actions, and desires, the outcome of which would determine the judgment of the Destroying Fate.

Of all this intrigue, in which he was soon to be involved, Roylands was quite ignorant, as he already had his plan of action sketched out. He would go to Melnos with Constantine Caliphronas, he would see this dream-woman in the flesh, and if she came up to his ideal, he would marry her, at whatever cost. Alas for the schemes of clever Mrs. Dengelton! they were all at an end, simply because a man had seen a pretty face, which he elevated into the regions of romance, and made attractive with strange mysteries of fanciful attributes. But Mrs. Dengelton did not know this, and, ignorance being bliss, still hinted to Maurice of matrimony, still threw him into the company of Eunice; while, as a checkmate to her plans, and to aid Crispin, Maurice still puzzled the good lady with hints of marriage one day, and neglect of Eunice the next. Eunice herself saw through it all, and was duly grateful to Maurice; so the only blind person was Mrs. Dengelton, who but perceived the delightful future that might be, not the disturbing present that was; if she had, her lamentations would have surpassed those of Jeremiah in bitterness and violence.

On such an important matter as going to the East in search of a mistress for Roylands Grange, Maurice felt naturally anxious to consult his old tutor, and accordingly one morning walked over to the Rectory, where he found Mr. Carriston as usual pottering about among his rose-trees. The hot sun of July blazed down on that garden of loveliness, and the sweet-smelling roses burned like constellations of red stars amid the cool green of their surrounding leaves.

'This is decidedly a rose-year,' said the good Rector approvingly, as he looked at the brilliance around him; 'I have never seen such a fine show of flowers. My nightingales should sing their sweetest here, if the tale of their love for the rose be true. Did you ever see such a glow of colour, Maurice?

> *Vidi Pæstano candere rosaria cultu*
> *Exoriente novo roscida Lucifero.*

But I don't think the poet saw finer roses than mine, even in Southern Italy.'

'"*Rosa florum regina est*,"' remarked Maurice, smiling.

'Eh! you match my quotation from Ausonius with a wretched little saying culled from your first

Latin reading-book. My dear lad, I am afraid my labour has been in vain, for your Latin is primitive.'

'No doubt it is,' assented Maurice cordially, 'but I have not the gift of tongues. I would that I had, as it will be necessary in the East.'

'The East!' repeated Carriston, sitting down under his favourite elm tree. 'What is this? Do you think of visiting the cradle of humanity?'

'Yes; the summer is nearly over, so like a swallow I wish to fly south to the blue seas of Greece.'

> '*Tous les ans j'y vais et je niche*
> *Aux métopes du Parthenon,*'

quoted the Rector genially. 'Do you know Gautier's charming poem? I wish I could go with you to see the land of Aristophanes.'

'Why not come?'

'Nay, I am too old a tree to be transplanted. The comedies alone must take me on the wings of fancy to Athens. What would my parishioners do without me? or my roses, for the matter of that? Still, I should like to be your travelling companion, and we could visit together those places which we read of in your days of pupilage. You will see Colonos, where the Sophoclean nightingales still sing; and the Acropolis of Athena Glaucopis, the ringing plains of windy Troy, and the birthplace of the Delian Apollo. Truly the youth of to-day are to be envied, seeing how easy travel has been made by steam. Happy Maurice! the Iron Age will enable you to view the Golden Age with but small difficulty.'

'Yes, it will greatly delight me to see all those famous places you have mentioned, sir; but I have a stronger reason.'

'Indeed! And that reason?'

'Is this.'

Maurice placed the portrait of Helena in the hands of his old tutor, and awaited in silence his next remark. Mr. Carriston adjusted his *pince-nez*, and gazed long and earnestly at the perfect beauty of the woman's countenance.

'"Is this the face that launched a thousand ships?"' he quoted from Marlowe; 'upon my word, I should not be surprised to hear it was. A beautiful woman, Maurice; she has the loveliness of the Argive Helen.'

'And the name also; she is called Helena.'

'Ah! then I understand she is a real woman?'

'Flesh and blood, according to Caliphronas.'

The Rector put down the picture with a sudden movement of irritation quite foreign to his usual courtly manner.

' I do not like Count Caliphronas,' he said abruptly
Did he give you this portrait ? '

' Yes.'

' Humph ! And may I ask whom it is intended
to represent ? '

' A Greek girl, called Helena, who lives in the
Island of Fantasy.'

' The Island of Fantasy ? ' repeated the Rector in
a puzzled tone.

' I mean the Island of Melnos, in the southern
archipelago of Greece.'

' How did it come by the extraordinary name of
Fantasy ? '

' Caliphronas called it so,' said Maurice carelessly.

There was silence for a few moments, and the
Rector rubbed his nose in a vexed manner, as he by
no means approved of the frequent introduction of
the Greek's name into the conversation, but hardly
saw his way to prevent it. At length he determined
to leave the matter in abeyance for the present, and
reverted to the question of Helena.

' Is it for the sake of this woman you are going to
the Levant ?' he asked, picking up the picture and
tapping it with his *pince-nez*.

' Yes.'

' Is this not rather a mad freak?'

Maurice did not answer for a moment, but moved uneasily in his seat; for, although he was quite prepared to be discouraged in his project by the Rector, he by no means liked the displeased tone in which he spoke. Mr. Carriston waited for an answer to his question, so Maurice was at length forced to give him one, and burst out into a long speech, so as to allow his tutor no opportunity of making any remark until he had heard all the views in favour of such Quixotism.

'I daresay it is a mad freak, sir, but not so very insane if you look upon it from my point of view. You know I have never been in love. True, I have always been fond of women and delighted in their society, but I have never had what you would call a passionate attachment in my life, nor did I think, until a few days ago, I was capable of such a thing. But when Caliphronas was sitting to me for Endymion, he happened to let fall that portrait, and told me it was one he had taken of a Greek girl at Melnos. As I admired the beauty of the face, he made me a present of the picture, and my admiration has merged itself in a deeper feeling, that of love. Oh, I know, sir, what you will say,

that such a passion is chimerical, seeing I have never
beheld this woman in the flesh, but I feel too strongly
on the subject to think I am the victim of a heated
imagination.   I love this woman—I adore her! she
is present with me day and night.   Not only her
face—no! It is very beautiful, but I can see below
that beauty.   She has a soul, a lovely pure soul,
which I worship, and I am anxious to see the actual
living, breathing woman, so as to make her my wife.'

'Your wife!   Are you mad, boy?'

'No, I am not mad, unless you call love a madness.
Oh, I know it is easy for one to advise calmly
on the woes of others.   But can you not feel for
me? You have been in love, Mr. Carriston, and you
know how such a passion overwhelms the strongest
man.   Caution, thought, restraint, prudence, are all
swept away by the torrent.   It is no use saying that
this passion I feel will pass, for I know it will not;
it is part of my life.   Till I die I shall see that face
before me, sleeping or waking.   Why, then, should I
pass the rest of my days in torture when I can alleviate
such mental suffering?   I am going to this unknown
island, I will see this unknown woman, and if she
comes up to the ideal being I have created from the
picture in my mind, I will marry her.   It may not be

wise, it may not be suitable; but it is, and will be, inevitable.'

The old man listened in astonishment to this lava-torrent of words which swept everything before it. He could hardly recognise his former calm-tempered pupil in this young man, whose flashing eyes, eloquent gestures, and rapid speech betrayed the strength of the passion which consumed him.

'"*Ira brevis est*,"' quoth the Rector wisely; 'I think love is the same.'

'My madness of love will last all my life—yes, for ever!'

'For ever is a long time.'

'Rector,' said Maurice entreatingly, 'what do you advise?'

'I advise nothing, dear lad,' replied Carriston quietly; 'what is the use of my giving advice which is opposed to your own desires, and therefore will be rejected?'

'True! true!' muttered Maurice, frowning. 'I must go to Melnos and convince myself of the truth of the matter. See here, sir, at present I am worshiping a creature of my own creation, with the face of that picture, but with the attributes of fancy. This chimera of the brain, as you will doubtless term her, haunts me night and day, so the only way to lay this feminine ghost is to see her in the flesh. She may be quite different to what I conceive, in which case I shall be cured of my fancy ; on the other hand, she may realise entirely my conception of beauty, purity, and womanliness : if she does, I will make her my wife, that is, of course, if she will have me for her husband.'

'As you put the matter in that light,' said Mr. Carriston, after a pause, 'I advise you to go to Melnos.'

'You do?'

'Decidedly! It is best to end this torture of the imagination, which I also know only too well. See this woman, if you like, but be sure she is all you desire her to be before making her your wife.'

'There is no fear that I shall let my heart govern my brain in such an important matter.'

'There is a great fear,' replied the Rector gravely, glancing at the picture; 'a young man's heart is not always under his control, and this woman has the beauty which inspires madness. Helen of Troy, Cleopatra of Egypt, Mary of Scotland, Ninon de l'Enclos of France, they were all Lamiæ, and their beauty was ever fatal to their victims.'

'Lovers,' corrected Maurice quickly.

'Victims,' reiterated Carriston firmly ; 'or, if you will, lovers, for the terms are synonymous.'

'Well, I will take your advice, sir, and go to the East in search of this lovely Helena of Melnos, but I promise you I will not be a victim.'

'I hope not, but I fear so.'

'You need not,' said Roylands gaily, delighted to have won over the Rector to his side. 'I shall come back alone, cured, or with a wife, and more in love than ever.'

'How will you find this island?'

'Oh, Caliphronas '—

'As beautiful and as false as Paris of Troy,' interrupted the Rector quickly, whereat Maurice shrugged his shoulders.

'Possibly he is, but I do not think I have anything to fear from him.'

'There is certainly no reason why he should be your enemy, yet I feel convinced he is so.'

'Why?'

'I cannot tell you unless I advance the Dr. Fell theory as an argument; but, to speak openly, my dear Maurice, this Greek seems to me to be like a sleek, soft-footed panther, beautiful to look on, but dangerous to meddle with.'

'I am not going to meddle with him. He is simply returning to his home in Greek waters, and I go with him. After we reach Melnos, very likely he will return to Ithaca.'

'Perhaps.'

'My dear old tutor,' cried the young man, laughing, 'you are full of fears, first of this Helena, again of this Greek. Ten to one I shall find both equally harmless.'

'I trust so; but I do not like your travelling alone with this Count Constantine.'

'I am not going to do so. Crispin is coming also.'

'Ah!' said Carriston in a satisfied tone; 'I am glad of that, for I like that young man very much. I am sure he is an honourable, straightforward fellow.'

'You are inconsistent. His life is as mysterious as that of Caliphronas, yet you trust the one and mistrust the other.'

'I do; it is a matter of instinct. Well, here is your Helena; I hope you will find the original as beautiful as the picture.'

'I hope so too,' answered Maurice, restoring the photograph to his pocket.

'By the way,' observed the Rector abruptly, 'what about Eunice?'

'Oh, she will not mourn me, for she has already consoled herself with Crispin.'

'Humph! I thought as much; and what does your aunt say?'

'She says nothing because she knows nothing.'

'Do you think that is wise?'

'No, I do not; so I am going to ask Crispin to explain who he is, what he is, and all about himself, before he leaves with me for the East. If his replies are satisfactory, I shall try and persuade my dear aunt to consent to the match; but you may depend upon it, my dear Rector, that if I find anything wrong with our poet, I will do my best to prevent his marriage with my cousin.'

'That is as it should be, but I fancy you will find Crispin an honest man.'

'You seem quite taken with him.'

'Yes; I am curiously drawn to that young man. Why, I do not know; but, from the frequent conversations I have had with him, he seems very honest and good-hearted, whereas your handsome Greek is, I am convinced, a worthless scamp.'

'Well, we shall see how your predictions are fulfilled.   But I must be off,' continued Maurice, glancing at his watch, 'it is past one o'clock.   Will you not come over to luncheon with me?'

'What! and leave my roses, which need water in this hot sun!   Go away, sir, and don't ask impossibilities.'

Maurice laughed and went away, while the Rector returned to his roses, and thought over the interview. He was doubtful as to the result of Maurice's quest for a wife, but, knowing the sterling good sense and honourable nature of his pupil, judged it best to let him take his own way.

'Every man must dree his weird,' said Carriston, watering-pot in hand.   'However this journey turns out, it will do Maurice good, for if it does not gain him a wife, it will at least banish the evil spirit which is spoiling his youth.'

Meanwhile the object of this soliloquy was striding up the avenue of the Grange at a rapid pace, and whistling gaily, out of sheer light-heartedness.   Never before had he felt so happy, a circumstance which suddenly made him pause in his lilting, as he thought of the saying of an old Scotch nurse.

'I hope I am not fey,' he said to himself; 'surely this joy does not prognosticate sorrow.   No; I will

not look on it in that gloomy light. I am going in
search of Helena,—Cœlebs in search of a wife,—and if
I find her as lovely as she seems to be, why, then '—

And he began whistling again, from sheer inability
to express his feelings in cold, measured words. As
he neared the house, the rich tenor voice of Caliphronas rang vibrating through the still air. His
song was, as usual, one of those Greek fragments he
was so fond of singing, and even the modern Greek
tongue, debased by centuries of foreign influences,
sounded pliable and liquid as the vowelled words
soared upward like swift-darting swallows. How
bare and bleak seems the translation, bereft of its
Hellenic sonorousness of speech !—

I will sail in a beakèd ship, impelled by rowers,
Over the waters to westward, where Helios sinks nightly in
* splendour,*
And there in a hidden island of dreams
Shall I see my belovèd smiling with starry eyes.
Her arms will enfold me—oh, they will clasp me so closely,
I will kiss her lips which burn like scarlet of sunset,
Till the nest of our love will flow over—flow over,
With delicate singing, and sighings of lover to lover.'

Caliphronas was standing on the steps of the
terrace, with his classic face uplifted to the serene
sky and, as he sang the song, with his hand resting
lightly on the white marble vase near him, he looked
the incarnation of blooming adolescence.

'Ha!' he cried, as Roylands nimbly mounted the steps; 'I was just wondering where you were. What have you been doing, Mr. Maurice?'

'I have been talking to the Rector, and for the last few moments I have been watching you, my Attic nightingale. Modern costume spoils you, Caliphronas, as it would spoil any one, so hideous is it. You should be draped in white robes, bear an ivory lyre, and minister to Apollo the Far-Darter.'

'Alas!' sighed the Greek, with sudden sadness in his eyes; 'Pan is dead, and with him Apollo. I have been born too late, for my soul is Athenian, and longs for the plane trees of Ilissus. But enough of this classicism, and tell me why you look so merry.'

'Because I have made up my mind to go with you to Melnos.'

Caliphronas smiled in an enigmatic manner, and sang two lines from his song,—

> *' And there in a hidden island of dreams*
> *Shall I see my belovèd smiling with starry eyes.'*

'What do those words mean?' asked Maurice abruptly.

'Ah, that you will know when we reach Melnos!'

CHAPTER XI.

THE CREED OF A MOTHER-IN-LAW.

In all good faith I do believe
That sons-in-law their wives deceive;
So, seeing marriage is a snare,
My daughter needs her mother's care;
And if this couple young be wise,
Their life they'll let me supervise.
For I can show the wife the way
To make the servants her obey,
Nor fail the husband's acts to see,
And rob him of his midnight key,
Improve his faults with frown and snub,
Insist he should give up his club;
And if he's an obedient boy,
His home will be a place of joy.
Thus ruling husband, home, and wife,
I shall secure a home for life.

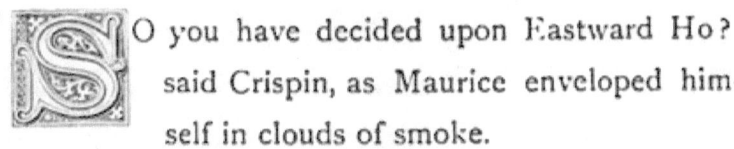O you have decided upon Eastward Ho?'
said Crispin, as Maurice enveloped him-
self in clouds of smoke.

They were seated in the smoking-room by themselves, for the ladies had long since retired; and

Caliphronas, unable to bear the fumes of tobacco, which, he averred, made his eyes sore and his head swim, had just gone off to bed.   Thus, left to that sweetest hour of the night which is somewhere about the stroke of twelve P.M., the poet and his host had established themselves in two comfortable arm-chairs, and, each armed with a pipe, were incensing the Muse of Fancy, who is frequently invoked by such worship. But the talk of the two was anything but fanciful, as they were engaged in discussing their projected tour in Levantine waters.   Maurice was rather glad Caliphronas retired so early, as he was anxious to have a quiet conversation with Crispin, and what better time or place could he have, than nearly midnight in the smoking-room, with the soothing weed, and the exhilarating whisky diluted with soda, to stimulate the drowsy brain.

It is wonderful how men at this mystic hour unbosom themselves to one another, and tell secrets which they certainly would not reveal in the daytime. Maurice knew this peculiarity of midnight confabulations, and perhaps thought that Crispin would take him into his confidence; but if he did think so he was disappointed, for Crispin kept his own counsel and held his tongue, save indeed to talk generally

about things with which Maurice was already well
acquainted.

'So you have decided upon Eastward Ho?' said
Crispin for the second time, finding that Maurice did
not reply immediately, which negligence was due to
the fact that he wished to speak to the poet about
Eunice, and was doubtful of the wisdom of such a
step. The second time of asking this question, however, roused him from his musings, and he answered
at once.

'Yes. I had a conversation with the Rector this
morning, and I have decided to travel abroad for a
year or so.'

'Do you mean a general tour of the world, or a
special part?'

'A special part. I am going to Greece.'

'Oh! The mainland or the islands?'

'The latter.'

'In that case, I know where you are going,' said
Crispin, carefully shaking the ashes out of his pipe;
'your destination is the Island of Melnos.'

'It is,' replied Maurice in some surprise. 'Do you
know Melnos?'

'Very well. I also know the woman you are going
to see.'

'Helena? How do you know that? I have told you nothing about it.'

'No; but Caliphronas mentioned something about your spiritual passion for that picture.'

This was mere guess-work, as Caliphronas had mentioned nothing of the sort; but Crispin was so well aware of the deep game which the Greek was playing, that he had no difficulty in arriving at a fair conclusion concerning his tactics. Maurice was, however, ignorant of Crispin's knowledge, and at once assumed that Caliphronas had been discussing his passion for this pictured Helena with the poet, perhaps laughing at it, and his pride was up in arms at once.

'Caliphronas has no right to speak to you about my private affairs,' he said angrily. 'I intended to tell you myself, but now he has forestalled me. I did not know he was such a gossip.'

'Nor is he. I said he told me, and so he did, indirectly; but if I did not know Caliphronas, Helena, and Melnos, I should still be in the dark concerning your projected journey.'

'Where is this Island of Fantasy?'

Crispin looked up with a quick smile.

'Oh, he told you the name Justinian calls it! The Island of Fantasy in imagination, and Melnos in reality, is situated in the southern portion of the Ægean Sea, beyond Paros, beyond Amorgos, nay, even beyond Anapli. As a matter of fact, it is an island little known, hidden, and, to speak exactly, in the Cretan Sea, between Telos and Crete.'

'I thought I was rather good at geography, but I never heard of the Island of Melnos before. Has it anything to do with the Island of Melos?'

'No; that is more to the north. But I do not wonder at your ignorance, as Melnos is known only to the sailors and shepherds who are thoroughly acquainted with that portion of the Archipelago.'

'What kind of an island is it?'

'A mountain—a volcanic mountain, extinct of course for the present, though I should not be surprised if it blew up one day and sent Justinian flying into the air with all his subjects.'

'Is this Justinian a king, that you talk about his subjects?'

'Well, a kind of minor king, such as Odysseus might have been. I know him very well.'

'And Helena?'

'Is his daughter.'

'His daughter!' repeated Maurice gravely. 'Is she as beautiful as this portrait shows her to be?'

'I should say more so,' replied Crispin, taking the photograph. 'Here you only get absolute stillness ; the great charm of Helena lies in the changeful expression of her face, and in her bright manner. Yes, she is altogether charming, and I do not wonder you have fallen in love with her face, even though this photograph fails to do justice to the original.'

In spite of his passion for Helena, which should have made him delight in these praises of her beauty, Maurice did not pay much attention to Crispin's speech, as he was thinking deeply, and the current of his thoughts was indicated by his next remark.

'Crispin, you said Caliphronas was merely a chance acquaintance you met at Athens ; but, so far as I can judge from the hints you drop, I believe you know him very well.'

'That is the real truth,' replied Crispin, without flinching. 'I did meet this Greek at Athens, but I knew him before that—in Melnos. Oh, I can tell you many things which would astonish you, but I cannot do so yet.'

'Why not ?'

'Because I have strong reasons for such reticence,' said the poet coldly ; 'either trust me all in all or not at all. This journey you are undertaking means more than you think, but I will not fail you, and as long as I am by your side you will take no hurt.'

'Are we in the Middle Ages? Is Caliphronas a freebooter, that you talk as if I were in danger?'

'I will explain all some day, and you will be rather astonished at my story.'

'I suppose there is nothing wrong in your story?'

'No. When I tell all about myself and my past life, I think it will satisfy not only you—but Mrs. Dengelton.'

'It is on her account that I made that rather rude remark, for, unless you can prove your name, your position, and your income to be satisfactory, she will never consent to your marriage with Eunice.'

'As to my name,' said Crispin, colouring a little at such plain speaking, 'I hope to prove that spotless, my position will be beyond reproach, and my income is larger than your own.'

'You are wealthy, then?'

'I am certainly well off, and I will give you my story at some later date, but at present I will answer no more of your questions.'

'And Mrs. Dengelton?'

'I am going to speak to her to-morrow morning, so as to put things right before I leave England. Oh, I

am not afraid of being absent.   Eunice loves me, and
will be true, while as to her mother, I can win that
lady on to my side, and will do so to-morrow.'

'You are an enigma, Crispin.'

'I am ; but, as I said before, I can explain myself
to your satisfaction, and intend doing so when I
consider it wise.   But you must trust me.'

'I do trust you.'

'I am afraid you ask too many questions, for
absolute trust,' said the poet dryly, relighting his pipe.

'I will ask you no more—save one.'

'Well?'

'Is Caliphronas to be trusted?'

'So long as I am with you, yes.'

'Ah, you have some power over him?'

'Now you are asking questions again.'

'I beg your pardon ; but do tell me about Caliphronas!'

Crispin paused for a moment, as if to consider how
he should reply to this remark.

'Caliphronas,' he said at length slowly, 'is a man
who is a slave to his own vices, and gratifies himself
at all costs.   He lets no one stand in the way of such
self-gratification ; but whether you are an obstacle or
not remains to be seen.   At all events, you have

elected to trust me, mysterious as I am, and I promise you on my word of honour that you shall have no reason to regret that trust. I foresee difficulties ahead, but these you need not be afraid of as long as I am by your side. You will leave Roylands with me, and you will return with me, and I give you my word you will not be a bit the worse for your journey, nay, I hope you will be the better.'

'One would think we were going to Timbuctoo, the way you talk,' said Maurice crossly. 'You have no idea how these enigmatic speeches pique my curiosity.'

'Well, such curiosity I will gratify—shortly.'

'But'—

'You said you would trust me, and ask no more questions.'

'I do trust you, and I will not.'

Certainly he could not complain of a lack of interest in life now: this mysterious woman Helena, these equally mysterious individuals, Crispin and Caliphronas,—all three riddles. Surely the son of Laius was never so bothered by enigmas as was this young country squire. However, it added new zest to the wine of life, and gave him something to look forward to, so on the whole Maurice was enjoying himself.

'By the way,' said Crispin lazily, after a pause, 'how are you going to Melnos?'

'Oh, I don't know exactly. Go by train to Venice, I suppose, and take an Austrian Lloyd steamer from there, or leave Marseilles by the French packet which goes to Athens. Once at the Piræus, there won't be much difficulty in exploring the Archipelago in search of your Island of Fantasy. To tell you the truth, however, as I only made up my mind this morning, I have not yet looked up routes, steamers, and all that sort of thing, but intend to go to town next week and find out all about them.'

'There will be no need,' said Crispin quietly; 'you can come to Greece in my yacht.'

'Your yacht! Why, I did not know you had one.'

'I know you didn't. Because I am a poet, you necessarily think I am poor, which is a mistake. I am sufficiently well off to keep a hundred and fifty ton steam yacht, which is at present lying at Southampton, ready to start when I wish. A poet and a yacht sound incongruous, I admit; and I suppose I am the first rhyme-stringer who ever possessed such an article, unless you except Shelley's boat partnership with Trelawny. But that was a small boat; my craft

is a genuine steam yacht, and in it I explore unknown
seas. You look astonished.'

'I am astonished. You are a poet-millionaire.'

'Not quite so wealthy as that, and I need hardly
tell you I did not pay for the yacht out of my poems.
But, of course, you will come with me to Greece in
The Eunice.'

'*Eunice?*'

'Yes; she was called *The Aphrodite*, but I re-
christened her *The Eunice* out of compliment to—
you know who.'

'Have you any more surprises in store?'

'Plenty,' replied Crispin, rising with a yawn; 'but
this one is quite enough to keep you awake for a
night. Oh dear, I am so sleepy!'

'Wait a minute. Does Caliphronas know you are
a yacht-owner?'

'No; I expect he will be surprised and confoundedly
jealous.'

'Jealous! Why?'

'Because he thinks all the good things of this life
should go his way. But you have not yet given me
your answer.'

'Oh, I will come by all means.'

'And so will our mutual friend, the Greek. What

a happy family we shall be! Well, good-night. I wish Eunice was coming in her namesake.'

' And Mrs. Dengelton,' said Maurice mischievously, lighting his candle.

' No; in my wildest dreams I never wished that. She would want to be captain of the ship. However, I am going to astonish my future mother-in-law to-morrow; so I must take a good night's rest, and husband my strength for the encounter. Good-night, once more.'

' Good-night, Crispin.'

They retired to their respective rooms, and Maurice fell asleep wondering who Crispin was, from what source he derived wealth enough to keep a yacht, and what connection he had with Caliphronas. All these things mixed together in his drowsy brain until the real world faded away, and he dreamed he was at Melnos, trying, like another Paris, to carry off Helena, while Caliphronas, in the guise of Menelaus, prevented such elopement.

Next day the brilliant sun had disappeared, and there was a grey veil of clouds drawn across the sky, which neutralised the brilliant tints of the summer's luxuriance of foliage and flowers. Caliphronas, ever impressionable to atmospheric changes, shivered at the dreary look which now spread over the earth, and it needed all his animal spirits to sustain his normal condition of careless joy. Even then he lacked his ordinary exuberance of life, and it appeared as if a great portion of his vitality disappeared with the sun.

'St. Theodore!' he said to Mrs. Dengelton, as they looked out of the window at the grey landscape ; 'do you often have this weather here?'

'No, not often,' she replied in a tone of regret ; 'I wish we did.'

'What! this dullness, this melancholy, this want of colour!'

'Why, my dear Count, it is a most beautiful day !' cried the lady, with great vivacity ; 'what have you to complain of?'

'Complain of?' The Greek's face was a study as he repeated her words, and he stared at her in surprise. 'Why, I complain of this want of sunlight ; it is not like yesterday, which was passable.'

'Passable!' echoed Mrs. Dengelton, surprised in her turn. 'Why, Count, since you have come to Roy-lands, the weather has been simply perfection. How long have you been in England?'

'Two months.'

'Then you must have had this lovely weather all

the time. You are an exceptionally lucky man, Count Constantine, for you have seen England at her best.'

'Why, have you worse days than this?' asked Caliphronas, with a shudder.

'Infinitely worse,' said Eunice, who at this moment joined them with Crispin : 'fog, snow, rain, hail, mist —oh, you don't know the capabilities of the English climate!'

'I am glad I am going away,' observed Caliphronas, with a sigh of relief; 'this place would kill me. Grey skies, small cultivated landscapes, ugly cities, sad-looking men and women. Oh, great saints! what do you know of life or pleasure?'

'I assure you, my dear Count,' began Mrs. Dengelton sweetly, 'that in the season'—

'What is the season?'

'The London season, which begins in May.'

'Oh, that is what I have seen. Up all night, tired all day, crowded rooms, unhealthy dinners, plenty of talk about nothing, and no rest—is that what you call the season? is that what you term life? St. Theodore! let me go back to Greece, there at least I can live.'

'But Greece is not like London,' said Crispin, with the intention of provoking the Greek.

'No, thank the saints, it is not, as you know well, Mr. Crispin; there, at least, are fresh air, laughing seas, wide plains, lofty mountains—one can breathe there—one can live and delight in living; but here— oh, pardon me, I cannot talk of it. I must go to Mr. Maurice for the Endymion, and I am glad I leave your dull greyness soon.'

When Caliphronas with this parting shot had vanished, Mrs. Dengelton turned to Crispin with a pitying smile.

'What an impulsive creature, is he not, Mr. Crispin? To talk about such barbaric lands, and call existence there life! Ah, he does not know what enjoyment is.'

'I think he does in his own way,' replied Crispin dryly, thinking of the difference between the free, open-air existence of the one, and the narrow, petty life of the other.

'Well, of course, you know a blind man never misses colour because he does not know what he loses,' said the lady apologetically. 'That poor dear Count is in exactly the same plight. Eunice, my dear, I wish you would go and write that letter to Lady Danvers at once. I want it to catch the noon-day post. We go to Lady Danvers when we leave here,' she added, as Eunice left the room. 'For my part, I would have been glad to have stayed here till the autumn, but dear Maurice has been ordered abroad for his health.'

'Yes, I know he is going,' said Crispin coolly; 'he is coming with me.'

'Coming with you?' repeated Mrs. Dengelton indignantly, wondering at the presumption of this, as she thought, poor poet.

'Yes,' replied Crispin equably, as he prepared to startle the lady; 'he is going to the East in my yacht.'

'Your yacht!' gasped Mrs. Dengelton, in the same tones in which she would have said, 'Your throne!' 'I did not know you—you'—

'Were rich enough to possess one,' said Crispin dryly, seeing the lady hesitated. 'Oh, I have had a yacht for many years. I hope you and Miss Dengelton will do me the favour of coming for a cruise in her some day.'

'Oh, I should be delighted!' cried Mrs. Dengelton, with a shudder, for she was a very bad sailor; 'but does it not take a great deal of money to keep up such an expensive luxury?'

'A great deal,' assented the poet, suppressing a smile as he saw the dexterous way in which Mrs.

Dengelton was trying to find out the extent of his income; 'but, fortunately, I can afford it.'

'How lucky you are!' sighed the lady, now adopting a more polite tone towards this wealthy young man. 'Ah, it is a splendid thing to be rich. My late husband was of good birth, but poor, and he did not leave me very well off. However, I have a sufficiently good income to live comfortably, and of course my dear daughter for a companion.'

'What will you do when Miss Dengelton marries?'

'Oh, I shall live with her still. You see, young wives are inexperienced, and I could take all household cares on my shoulders.'

Crispin shuddered, for the prospect of living under the same roof with this lady was anything but an inviting one.

'Of course, I do not mind speaking freely to you, dear Mr. Crispin,' pursued Mrs. Dengelton, determined to crush all thoughts Crispin might have regarding Eunice, 'because you are such a friend of dear Maurice. You know I wish him to marry his cousin, it would be a perfect match.'

'Would it?' said Crispin grimly.

'Yes; it would keep the property in the family,' said Mrs. Dengelton, who had arrived at this remarkable conclusion by some means known only to herself; 'and then, of course, this would be my home, and I could live here with my dear children. You see, I speak openly to you, because I know you would like to see dear Maurice happily married.'

'I would indeed, Mrs. Dengelton, but not to your daughter.'

'Indeed, Mr. Crispin! and why not?'

'Because I want to marry her myself.'

'Mr. Crispin!'

If a bombshell had dropped through the roof, Mrs. Dengelton could not have been more astonished. She half guessed that this audacious poet admired Eunice, but to speak thus so boldly, and after she had given her views as to the future settlement of her daughter in matrimony—it was too horrible! Who was this man? Nobody knew. He had not even two names like respectable people, and to propose to bestow the only one he possessed on her daughter, was too much for Mrs. Dengelton's powers of endurance. She was actually dumb with astonishment, and those who had once heard this lady's tongue could have seen from that alone how thunderstruck she was. For a minute she gazed at Crispin with horror-struck eyes, but as he did not turn into stone before that Medusa gaze, or even have the grace to blush, Mrs. Dengelton recovered her powers of speech with a weak laugh.

'Oh, of course you are jesting!'

'I am not jesting. I wish to marry your daughter.'

'Impossible!'

'Why is it impossible?'

'Oh, because—because'— Mrs. Dengelton could not really bring herself to give the real reasons, so fenced dexterously,—'Because, you see, I wish her to marry her cousin, and keep the property in the family.'

'The property will remain in the family without such a marriage,' said Crispin provokingly; 'and as for your daughter, she does not love Maurice.'

'Not love Maurice!' screamed Mrs. Dengelton wrathfully.

'No, she loves me.'

'Loves you!' gasped the good lady faintly, feeling for her smelling-salts. 'Oh, this is some horrible dream!'

'By no means,' replied Crispin quietly; 'I really do not see why you should make such an uncomplimentary remark. I love your daughter, and I wish to marry her. Is there anything extraordinary in that?'

' Eunice could marry any one.'

' No doubt, but she will not. I am the only man she will marry.'

' Indeed! You forget her mother's consent is necessary.'

' At present, yes, because she is under age—but afterwards '—

' Eunice Dengelton will obey me all her life,' said the lady furiously ; ' and I will never, never consent to her marriage with you, sir ! '

' Why not ? '

' Because I do not know who you are,' retorted Mrs. Dengelton tartly.

' I will satisfy you on that point before the marriage.'

' Then I do not know if you can support a wife.'

' If I can support a yacht, I can certainly support a wife,' said Crispin ironically ; ' but if you want me to be exact as to figures, my income is twelve thousand a year.'

' Twelve thousand a year ! ' gasped Mrs. Dengelton in amazement ; ' why, you are richer than Maurice ! '

' Yes, twice as rich. Is there any other question you would like to ask ? '

' Well, I should like to know about your parents.'

' I have no parents. I am an orphan.'

' And where do you come from, Mr. Crispin ? '

' From the East.'

'Heavens!' cried Mrs. Dengelton, as a dreadful thought struck her; 'you are not a Hindoo, or a negro, or a Hottentot ? '

'Well, I am certainly dark,' replied the poet, laughing, 'but I am, as it happens, a pure-blooded Englishman. But come now, Mrs. Dengelton, I have answered your questions, so in common fairness you must answer mine. Will you let me marry your daughter ? '

' I—I—really I don't know what to say,' said Mrs. Dengelton, unwilling to let the chance of such a wealthy match slip, and yet doubtful as to the position of the suitor. 'I must think it over. Tell me who you are ? '

' Not now. I will satisfy you fully concerning my family when I return from Greece.'

'Ah! am I right in saying you are going to the East to see your relatives about this marriage ? ' said Mrs. Dengelton archly.

'Partly right. I am going as much on your nephew's account as my own.'

' And what is *he* going for ? '

'That I cannot tell you, Mrs. Dengelton,' replied

Crispin mendaciously, 'you must ask him that your-self. But as to this marriage'—

'I cannot give you an answer now—really I cannot.'

'Will you give me an answer when I return from the East?'

'When will you return?'

'In three months.'

'Yes, I will give you an answer then,' said Mrs. Dengelton glibly, having quite determined to throw Crispin over, should she meet with a more desirable match for her daughter. Crispin guessed this double dealing, and at once met the feminine plot by a masculine counterplot.

'Mrs. Dengleton,' he said solemnly, 'I love your daughter, and she loves me. When I return in three months from the East, I will satisfy you on all points you desire to know. If these questions you ask are answered to your complete satisfaction, will you agree to our marriage?'

'Yes,' replied Mrs. Dengelton, all the volubility frightened out of her, 'I will.'

'Then give me your word that during my absence you will not try and induce your daughter to marry any one else.'

'I hardly think it is necessary to ask that,' said the

lady, with dignity, though in her heart of hearts she knew it was very necessary, as also did Crispin, who still pressed his request.

'Perhaps it is not necessary; still, I would like your word for it that such a thing will not occur.'

'Well, well, I promise,' replied Mrs. Dengelton peevishly, rising to her feet. 'What a pertinacious man you are, Mr. Crispin! Mind, I will not consent to this marriage unless I am thoroughly satisfied about your position, income, and family.'

'I will satisfy you on all those points,' rejoined Crispin, with a bow, as he held the door open for her to pass through.

'I feel quite upset,' said the good lady, as she hastily departed. 'I am sure I don't know what Maurice will say.'

'I do,' thought Crispin, as he closed the door; 'he will be delighted. I talk very confidently, but I am doubtful. Position—yes, that is all right, I am a poet; money—well, she can hardly complain of twelve thousand a year, safely invested; family—ah, that is the difficulty! I wonder if I can get the truth out of Justinian, he alone knows. I cannot marry with only one name, but I will have two before I return from Melnos, or else '—

He paused, and struck his fist hard against his open hand.

'I will force Justinian to tell me,' he muttered between his clenched teeth. 'I also hold cards in this game he is playing, and even with him and Caliphronas as adversaries I shall win. Maurice Roylands is Justinian's stake, Helena is the stake of Caliphronas, as he chooses to call himself; but Eunice is mine, and with such a prize to gain I am desperate.'

His eyes fell on an open volume of Thomas à Kempis, which Mrs. Dengelton, in strange contrast to her usual worldliness, was fond of reading, and he saw the following sentence:—

'Love desires to be aloft, and will not be kept back by anything low and mean.'

'I accept the omen,' he said, closing the book slowly. 'I desire Eunice, and no lowness or meanness on the part of Justinian and Andros will keep me back. I accept the omen.'

CHAPTER XII.

THE NEW ARGONAUTS.

From distant isles of tropic blooms,
Enthroned on seas of hyaline,
Across the waters smaragdine,
The weak winds waft us faint perfumes
Of incense, musk, and fragrant balms,
That shed their scents 'mid lasting calms,
Beneath the shade of bending palms.

These perfumes rouse lethargic brains
From idle dreams and visions pale.
As modern Argonauts we sail
Far o'er the trackless ocean plains ;
We wish no golden fleeces sleek,
But in these islands of the Greek,
A woman's lovely face we seek.

ALL preparations having been made, it was decided to start for Greece about the end of July ; and these modern Argonauts were in the highest spirits at the prospect of the coming voyage,—Caliphronas because his object was gained, and Roylands would soon be on his way to the Island of Melnos ; Crispin because he had come to a comfortable understanding with Mrs. Dengelton ; and Maurice for the simple reason that he was going to see in the flesh this beautiful vision of fancy which haunted his brain. The Grange was to be left to the guardianship of the housekeeper, and its master, giving up, at least for the present, a life of ease, was about to embark on one of those adventurous expeditions so dear to the hearts of our restless young Englishmen. Mrs. Dengelton and Eunice had arranged to stay with Lady Danvers in London, and the good old Rector still remained in his sleepy village, looking after his parishioners, his Aristophanic translation, and his beloved roses.

In company with Maurice, the poet had taken a journey to Southampton to see if the yacht was all in order for the projected voyage, and had stayed there three days to attend to all necessary matters. *The Eunice* was a beautiful little craft, schooner-rigged fore and aft, and was manned by an excellent crew ; so with all this luxury the three adventurers looked forward to having a very pleasant time. It was now the season when the halcyon broods on the waves, so they expected a smooth passage to Melnos, and as all three were capital sailors, even if they did have stormy weather they cared very little for such a possibility. Caliphronas, delighted at leaving this dull island for his own brilliant skies, was beside himself with delight, and talked incessantly of the pleasures in store for them on the Island of Melnos.

On the evening before they left England, Maurice invited the Rector to a farewell dinner; and the company assembled round the hospitable table of the Grange were very merry indeed, with perhaps the exception of Eunice, who was somewhat sad at the prospect of parting from her poet. The weather was still dull and grey, and it was only the prospect of a speedy departure that kept Caliphronas bright ; but as that departure took place next day, he was in the gayest spirits.

'We are the New Argonauts,' he said merrily, with the affectation of classicism which distinguished him ; ' we sail for the Colchian strand.'

' It is to be hoped we find no Medea there,' observed Crispin, with a smile.

'No ; our Medea is no sorceress, but a daughter of Venus, the modern Helen of Troy. Mr. Maurice is her Jason. You, Crispin, are Orpheus.'

'And you, Count?' asked Maurice, amused at this fancy.

'I?' said Caliphronas lightly. 'Well, I hardly know. Shall I say Hercules?'

'Or Hylas,' suggested the Rector idly.

'Neither !' interposed Crispin pointedly. 'We will

take a passenger from another famous ship, and call him Ulysses, the craftiest of the Greeks.'

Caliphronas frowned at this somewhat uncomplimentary remark, but immediately recovered his gaiety, and burst out laughing.

'Oh, I do not mind in the least. Ulysses, by all means. After all, he had some very pleasant times with Circe, Calypso, and such-like ladies.'

'You seem to know your Homer, Count,' said the Rector, rather surprised at the classical knowledge of this ignorant young man.

'Or his Lemprière,' muttered Crispin significantly.

Decidedly Crispin was not polite ; but, truth to tell, the prospect of a voyage in company with a man he disliked was almost too much for him, and it took him all his self-restraint to prevent him breaking out into open war against the Greek. Caliphronas knew this, but, appearing to take no notice of such a hostile attitude, resolved to bide his time, and make Crispin suffer for such insolence at the first opportunity. It seemed as though poor Maurice would not have a very pleasant time of it, cooped up in a vessel with these two enemies ; but, doubtless, when Crispin played host in his own yacht, he would treat the Count in a more courteous fashion.

This was exactly the view Crispin took of the matter ;

and as he knew, according to the laws of hospitality, he
would have to be scrupulously polite to Caliphronas
on board *The Eunice*, he was taking advantage of the
present time, and giving his humour full rein in the
direction of his real feelings. If he could only have
prevented Caliphronas coming, by such a display of hostility, he would have been very glad, as he mistrusted
the Greek very much; but Caliphronas was impervious
to the shafts of irony, and, as long as he gained his
ends, did not care what was said to him or of him.
This brilliant stranger was a man entirely without
pride, and would put up with any insults rather than
jeopardise his plans by resenting such discourtesy. It
was the last opportunity Crispin would have of showing his real feelings, so he took advantage of it; and
though it was scarcely gentlemanly of him to do so, the
Count was such an unmitigated scoundrel that honourable or courteous treatment was entirely lost on him.

However, Eunice overheard his ironical remarks,
and looked reproachfully at him, whereon Crispin
restrained his temper, and strove to be delightfully
amiable, no very easy task in his present frame of
mind. With this good resolve he talked as pleasantly
as he was able, and heard Caliphronas romance about
his fictitious life without contradicting him, which he
felt sorely inclined to do. It must not be forgotten

that Crispin had hitherto led a semi-civilised life, and had not acquired that knack of concealing his likes or dislikes so necessary in our artificial society; besides which he was a very honest-minded man, and, knowing the true story of Caliphronas, the deliberate lies, flashy manner, and snake-like subtlety of the Greek annoyed him.

Maurice also distrusted the Count, especially after his conversation with Crispin regarding the real name, career, and character of the man; but, being more versed in the science of deception, behaved admirably towards his guest in every way, thereby deceiving Caliphronas into taking all this enforced suavity for actual good-fellowship. As to the Rector, he was extremely punctilious in his behaviour, and neither by word nor deed showed his dislike of this sleek-footed panther, who was about to bear away his favourite Maurice into unknown dangers.

'You must bring us all kinds of things from Greece, Maurice,' said Mrs. Dengelton in her usual gushing manner. 'I adore foreign ornaments—those silver pins, you know, like Italian women wear, and Moorish veils, and Algerian lamps—so delightful—they fill up a room wonderfully.'

'Yes, and make it look like a curiosity-shop,' replied Maurice, laughing. 'Oh, my dear aunt, you

may depend on my bringing you all kinds of out-
landish things ; but as to Italian pins, Moorish veils,
Algerian lamps, I don't suppose I shall find any of
those sort of things in Greece.'

' What shall I bring you ? ' asked Crispin, as he held
open the door for Eunice to pass through.

They were beyond the hearing of the table, Mrs.
Dengelton had sailed on ahead to the drawing-room,
so they were virtually alone.

' What shall I bring you ? ' he asked in a whisper.

' Yourself,' she replied in the same tone. And
Crispin returned to his seat with the delightful con-
viction that Eunice was the most charming girl in the
world, and he was certainly the most fortunate of poets.

The Rector poured himself out a glass of his
favourite port, and began to converse with Caliphronas ; while Maurice and Crispin, lighting their
cigarettes, chatted about the yacht, her sea-going
powers, the question of stores, the anticipated time
she would take to run down to the Ægean, and such-
like marine matters.

' Shall you pay us another visit, Count ? ' asked the
Rector, more for the sake of starting a conversation
than because he really cared about such a possibility.

' No, I do not think so. I am going to be married
and settle down in my own island.'

'Ithaca?'

Caliphronas laughed a little on hearing the name.

'Yes; on Ithaca.'

'Are you a politician?'

'I? No. I care not two straws for the recon-
struction of the Greek Empire, the recovery of
Byzantium from the Turks, or any of those things
which agitate my countrymen. No. I am a terribly
selfish man, sir, as you will doubtless think. I only
want to live in happiness, and for the good of my
fellow-creatures I care nothing.'

'Is that not rather an egotistical way of looking at
life?'

'Doubtless, sir, from your point of view, but not
from mine. You are a priest of your Church, what
we call a Papa in my country, and live the life of the
soul, while I live the life of the body. You believe
in self-abnegation—I in self-satisfaction. With this
beautiful world I am content, but you rack your soul
with longings for the life beyond the grave. In a
word, I am real, you are ideal ; but I am the happiest.'

'The happiness of the beasts which perish!' said
the Rector emphatically.

'Well, the beasts, as a rule, have a very good time
of it during their lives; as to the rest, we all perish at
last.'

' The body, but not the soul.'

' Ah, that I do not know. I may have a soul, but I am not certain ; but I have a body, and as long as that is at ease, why should I trouble about things in the next life ? '

' Do you ever think of the hereafter ? '

' Never! If I die, I die ! While I live, I live ! I prefer present certainty to future doubt.'

Mr. Carriston was silent, as he did not care about arguing theology with this subtle Greek, whose religion, whose philosophy assumed Protean forms to meet every objection. He was full of sophistry and double dealing, an unfair adversary in every sense of the word, and was so encased in his armour of self-complacency and egotism, that he could never be brought to look at things either spiritual or material in any other light than that which satisfied the selfishness of his own soul. The Rector, therefore, avoided the threatened argument, and applied himself to his wine, which was a much more agreeable task than attempting to convince this egoist that the supreme aim of life was not the pampering of the passions of the individual man.

' Apart from the theological aspect of the case,' said Carriston good-humouredly, ' it is rather a mistake to live only for one's self. " Where ignorance is bliss," I grant; but, because you know no higher life than that of the body, you at once assume that there can be no happier existence.'

'Oh, I do not say that,' answered Caliphronas lightly. 'No doubt you people who mortify the flesh, who listen to the voice of conscience, who consider the soul more than the body, and who look upon this life as a preparation for a future existence, are happy in your self-torturings. All that sort of thing came in with the first Christian century, and made the mediæval ages a hell of anguish; but I— I am a Greek—a pagan, if it please you—who look on this world not as a prison, but as a garden wherein to live happily. Your mourning Man of Sorrows is entirely opposed to our joyous Apollo; your gloomy views of life, to our serenity of temperament. The difference is plain: for you, a Christian, cannot understand the joyous songs of Paganism;—I, a pagan, shudder at your penitential psalms of Christianity. We should neither of us ever convince the other, therefore an argument which has not a common basis from which to start is unprofitable.'

' I am not going to argue,' replied Carriston, smiling, 'and I agree with you that arguments are unprofitable. Unless the change takes place in your own breast, it would be worse than useless for me to

attempt to reason with you. But you are evidently
not of the opinion of an Elizabethan ancestor of mine,
among whose papers I discovered the following lyric :

Oh, shall we pass contented days,
Unheeding Fortune's crown of bays,
Which decks the brows
Of those whose vows
Compel them to incessant strife
And restless life.

Ah no ; tho' pleasing to the sense,
This cloying life of indolence
But fills the soul
With weary dole,
And turns the sweet, which doth us bless,
To bitterness.'

'Your Elizabethan ancestor was not healthy-
minded,' said Caliphronas coolly ; 'if he had been
he would never have written such silly verses. It
is your unhealthy life, your unhealthy bodies, which
breed such restlessness in you.'

'At all events, that restlessness has made England
what she is,' replied the Rector, rather nettled at
the rudeness of the Greek.

'A land of money-worship, a land of noisy steam-
engines, a land of poverty and wealth—extremes in
both cases. Yes, I quite believe your restless spirit
has brought you to this satisfactory state of things.
Come, sir,' added the Count, with a charming smile,
seeing the Rector was rather annoyed, 'let us agree

to differ. For me, Greece—for you, England; for me, Nature—for you, Art. Two parallel straight lines cannot meet.'

Carriston laughed at this way of settling the question, but made no further remarks, and after a desultory conversation between all four gentlemen had ensued, they went into the drawing-room to join the ladies.

Mrs. Dengelton was engaged on her everlasting fancy-work; and Eunice, with a rather disconsolate look on her face, was idly turning over the pages of a book. Crispin stole quietly behind her and glanced over her shoulder. It was a volume of his poems, and he felt flattered.

'And to think,' said Mrs. Dengelton, without further prelude, 'that you will be so far away from home to-morrow.'

'The world is my home,' cried Caliphronas gaily.

'We Englishmen are narrower in our ideas,' observed Maurice dryly; 'we look on England as our home.'

'Ah, there's no place like home,' sighed the Honourable Mrs. Dengelton sentimentally.

'If by home you mean England, I am very glad of it,' retorted the Count audaciously; 'I would rather live in exile in Greece. But come, I will say no more evil things about your beloved island of fogs.'

'If you do, I shall sing "Rule Britannia,"' said Maurice, laughing.

'What is that?'

'Our national song. Do you know any national songs of your country?'

Caliphronas smiled with an expression of supreme indifference.

'Oh yes; but I don't think you would care about them. Besides, most of my songs are of love and wine.'

'Oh!' said Mrs. Dengelton in a shocked tone; 'really, Count, you say the most dreadful things!'

'Other times other manners,' observed the Rector humorously. 'Horace, for instance, said things which would shock you, my dear Mrs. Dengelton.'

'I've no doubt about it,' retorted the lady viciously; 'but, thank heaven, I do not know Latin.'

'But you know French, aunt,' said Maurice wickedly; 'and I am afraid Gyp, George Sand, and Belot, are quite as bad, if not worse, than the Latin poet.'

'Maurice,' replied Mrs. Dengleton severely, unable to parry this attack, 'remember your cousin is in the room.'

'I beg your pardon, aunt.'

'And now, Count Caliphronas,' said the good lady, thus appeased, 'suppose you sing us one of your songs.'

'I am afraid it will shock you,' replied the Count slyly.

'Oh dear no! none of us know Greek.'

'That is hardly complimentary to me, who have given up all my life to the study of the Greek poets.'

'I don't mean you, Rector, but the young people.'

'Oh, I do not mind singing,' said Caliphronas, going to the piano; 'if the words of my songs were translated, you would find them very harmless. They only contain the language of love known to all the world.'

'Shall I play for you?' asked Crispin, looking up from the poem he was reading to Eunice.

'If you would be so kind.'

'What will you sing?' said the poet, sitting down at the piano. 'No love, no wine to-night. It is our last meeting in England, so sing some song of parting.'

'Shall I sing "The Call to Arms"?'

'Yes, that will be stirring enough.'

Whereupon Caliphronas sang that patriotic song, which was written by some modern Hellenic Tyrtæus during the War of Independence. Crispin afterwards translated it into the metre of Byron's famous 'Isles of Greece' for the benefit of Eunice, who was anxious to know the words which, clothed in their Greek garb, rang through the room like the inspiriting blare of a trumpet.

Thermopylæ! Thermopylæ!
  Give back your Spartan sons of yore,
To raise the flag of liberty,
  And dye its folds in Turkish gore;
Then will the crimson banner wave
Above the freeman, not the slave.

Arise, ye Greeks, and break your chains!
  By daring hearts is freedom won.
Behold, the Moslem crescent wanes
  Before the rising Attic sun;
Oh, let its golden beams be shed
On chainless Greeks, and tyrants dead!

Your fathers' swords were laurel-wreathed,
  And wielded well by freemen brave;
Why are your swords so idly sheathed,
  While Greece is still a Turkish slave?
Shall Hellas, Mother of the West,
In servitude ignoble rest?

Oh, shame! that it should come to this,
  When by your sides hang idle swords;
Arise, ye sons of Salamis,
  Whose fathers quelled the Persian hordes,
And drive the Moslem to the sea,
Till Hellas and her sons be free.

When the song was finished, Caliphronas turned away silently, and Carriston, who was seated near, saw to his astonishment that the eyes of the emotional Greek were suffused with tears.

'That man has some noble traits,' he said to himself as he noticed this; 'he is moved by the wrongs of his country.'

'What a fine ringing melody!' cried Eunice, whose eyes were flashing with excitement.

'It is like "Chevy Chase,"' said Maurice quickly, 'and stirs the heart like the sound of a trumpet.'

'The poet was evidently inspired by Byron,' remarked Crispin, idly fingering the piano keys; 'I expect he wrote it after the "Isles of Greece" song. Ah, a Greek should have written that.'

'I am afraid the days of Alcæus are past,' replied the Rector, who had understood a considerable portion of the song, owing to his acquaintance with the ancient Attic tongue; 'Greece prefers Anacreon. Still she won her freedom bravely.'

'And to what gain?' said Caliphronas bitterly; 'to be ruled by a Danish prince. Better the republics of Athens, Sparta, and Thebes, than such playing at monarchy.'

'To revive the ancient government you must have the ancient patriots, poets, and scholars.'

'That I am afraid is impossible. No, the glory has departed from Greece. Centuries of oppression have crushed the creative faculty out of her.'

'Oh, let us hope, when the Greek Empire is reconstructed, we shall have a new Pindar, a new Sophocles, a new Plato.'

'That is a dream of the lyre, not of the sword,'

replied Caliphronas, carelessly glancing at his watch.
' By the way, it is very late, and, as we have to be
up early, I suppose we ought to retire early.'

' I am quite with you, Count,' said Mrs. Dengelton,
rolling up her work. ' Come, Eunice, we must get
our beauty sleep.'

' Humph! the mother needs it more than the
daughter,' thought Crispin, but did not give vent to
this very uncomplimentary remark, and hastened to
give the ladies their candles.

' Are you going to bed, Caliphronas?' asked
Maurice, when the ladies had gone. ' We intend to
smoke.'

' Going to shorten your lives,' replied the Count,
smiling. ' No; I am like Mrs. Dengelton, I require
my beauty sleep;' and at that he also departed.

The Rector, in company with his two young
friends, went to the smoking-room, and had a
pleasant conversation, but it was noticeable that all
three gentlemen carefully avoided mentioning the
name of Caliphronas. Decidedly the Greek was not
in favour, and, in spite of the good impression he
had created in the Rector's mind by his patriotic
emotion, that gentleman showed how deeply rooted
was his distrust by his parting words to Crispin.

' Remember, I leave Maurice in your hands, Mr.

Crispin,' he said in a faltering voice ; 'he is very dear
to me, and you must protect him from all danger.'

'My dear Rector, I am not a child,' interposed
Maurice, rather nettled ; 'nor are we going to the
wilds of Africa.'

'You may meet with worse enemies than the
savage beasts of Africa,' replied the Rector obstin-
ately. 'I do not trust your friend Caliphronas.'

'Be content,' said Crispin, shaking the Rector
warmly by the hand, 'I will watch over Maurice ;
and as to Caliphronas, you need not be afraid of
him. I know the man.'

'And know any good of him ?'

'Ah, that is a secret at present ; but you may be
sure he will not harm Maurice while I am near.'

'One would think we were going into danger by
the way you talk,' said Roylands impatiently, 'instead
of for a pleasant cruise in Greek waters.'

'The New Argonauts,' observed the Rector, laughing. 'Good-night, Mr. Crispin. Good-night, my
dear lad ; come over and say good-bye to-morrow.'

The Argonauts promised, and the Rector, quite at
peace concerning his dear pupil, departed.

'You doubt Caliphronas ; the Rector doubts Caliphronas,' said Maurice, when the old man had gone.
'I am getting rather wearied of such doubts.'

'Well, I will set your doubts at rest in—say a week's time.'

'And are your revelations startling?'

Crispin shrugged his shoulders.

'Not very; it all depends upon what you call startling. Really I have made by my talk this molehill of a Caliphronas into a mountain of dissimulation and deceit. He is not a good man, but I have no doubt he is as good as his neighbours.'

'The mystery which environs him fascinates me.'

'No doubt; the unknown is always attractive,' replied Crispin sententiously. 'But after all, when I tell you everything, you may be disappointed. The mountain may only bring forth a mouse, you know. But, at all events, I look forward to some pretty lively times.'

'Where?'

'In the Island of Melnos. My dear innocent Englishman, you are being drawn into a network of intrigue and duplicity, but, as I hold all the threads in my hand, you will come out all right in the end.'

'You puzzle me! I hope I *shall* come all right out of this mystery.'

'I heard a vulgar saying at a music hall which applies to this case and to you,' said Crispin gaily; 'it was, "Keep your eye on your father, and your father will pull you through."'

CHAPTER XIII.

THE PAST OF A POET.

We all have histories. The meanest hind
Who turns the steaming furrow can unfold
Some story in his uneventful life,
Which stirs the wonderment of him who hears,
To thoughts bewildered, how so small a stage
Can thus contain so great a tragedy

HE EUNICE left Southampton on an un-
pleasantly wet day, and standing on the
deck, under a dull grey sky, the three
adventurers felt quite dispirited as they watched the
receding shores of England veil themselves in chilly
mists. Going down the Channel they had moderately fair weather, but no sunlight, and Caliphronas,
depressed by the sombre aspect of the scene, retreated to his cabin in a very miserable frame of
mind. Both Crispin and Maurice, however, less
sensitive to atmospheric influences, mostly remained
on deck watching the grey sea heave dully under
the grey sky. In the Bay of Biscay bad weather

prevailed as a matter of course, and the yacht tossed about a good deal in the choppy waters. Not until they passed the Straits did they have fine weather, for the first burst of sunlight showed them the giant rock of Gibraltar frowning on the left as they steamed rapidly into the blue waters of the Mediterranean.

Had Maurice so desired, Crispin was quite willing to put in for a day, but the young man was anxious to proceed to Melnos, and the yacht soon left the picturesque sentinel of the Mediterranean behind. The weather now became warm and bright, bringing Caliphronas out of his cabin again, like a brilliant butterfly, to bask in the sunshine. The arid island of Malta came in sight, and they saw its precipitous shores rising sternly from the tideless waters. For a few hours they cast anchor in the Grand Harbour, and went on shore to explore Valetta, with its steep streets, quaint houses, and mongrel population. An afternoon spent in leisurely strolling along the Strada Reale, and looking at the bizarre mixture of Turks, Jews, Arabs, Italians, and red-coated English soldiers, proved an agreeable change after their nine days' run from Southampton, and they re-embarked in much better spirits than when they left England. Now they were in tropical heat, with a cloudless sky above, and the brave little yacht steaming merrily across the glittering waters, leaving a trail of white foam behind her. Nearer and nearer they drew to the enchanted shores of Greece, and to glowing days succeeded by warm nights lighted by mellow constellations and delicately silver moons.

It was when they were in Adria, the ancient name of the sea between Sicily and Greece, that Crispin told Maurice the story of his life. Dinner was long since over, and the three gentlemen lounged on deck smoking the pipes of peace—that is, Crispin and Maurice smoked and lounged, for Caliphronas did neither the one nor the other, but paced restlessly about the deck, looking up into the darkly blue sky, and singing snatches of Greek songs.

' Do you see Taygetus, Mr. Maurice?' he said, pointing to the lofty snow-crowned range of mountains in the distance. ' This is your first glimpse of Greece, is it not? Yes, of course it is. I am sorry you do not find our shores bathed in sunlight to greet you; still yonder snowy mountain, this calm sea, that serene sky is beautiful, is it not?'

' Very beautiful.'

Whereat Caliphronas, leaning over the taffrail and looking dreamily at the shores of his native land, broke out into song.

'I would I were hunting on lofty Taygetus,
Which kisses the starry sky with snows of chastity,
Then might I meet the lost nymph
Who beloved by a god was set as a star on high,
But fell from thence, and was lost in the snowy wilderness.'

'Taygeta!' said Crispin, who knew the song well. 'Yes; she was one of the Pleiades, certainly; but I don't think she was the lost Pleiad, nor do I think she had anything to do with yonder mountain. If you hunted there, Caliphronas, you would meet Bacchus and his crew, but no nymph.'

'I sing the song as 'twas sung to me,' said the Count blithely, balancing himself on one foot. 'This is the land of fancy, not of fact; so why bring in your hard truths to destroy the glory of tradition. No; Taygeta haunts those hills, and if I wandered upward to the snows I would meet her.'

'If you saw a nymph you would go mad,' remarked Maurice, alluding to the old Greek superstition.

'I am mad now, Mr. Maurice,—mad with the scent of wind and wave and shore. Can you not smell the perfumes blowing from the land?'

'No; I'm sure I cannot, nor you either.'

'You are no believer. See, from the moonlit waters arise the Nereides to welcome us to the seas of Poseidon. Arethusa, Asia, and Leucothoe are all waving their white arms, and singing songs of the wondrous caves beneath the waves.'

'Ridiculous!' retorted Maurice stolidly.

'You are no idealist,' said Caliphronas petulantly. 'Dull Englishman as you are, the land of romance spreads her wonders in vain for you. Crispin, you are a poet; behold the daughters of the sea!'

Crispin smiled absently, and tossed his cigarette into the waters which rushed past, glittering in the moonlight with the greyish glint of steel.

'You forget this is no galley of Ulysses, my friend. A modern steamer, with a noisy screw beating the waters, is enough to scare away all the nymphs in the vicinity.'

'And this is a poet!' cried the Greek indignantly, addressing the stars; 'this dull-eyed being who can see no wonders in the seas! Oh, shade of Homer, conjure up for him the island nymph, Calypso, and her lovely train; conjure '—

'I think Homer will have to conjure up himself first,' said Crispin flippantly.

'Which he certainly will not do on the ocean,' added Maurice lazily; 'your mighty poet was a land-lubber.'

Caliphronas looked indignantly at them both, then went off in a rage.

' I will go and have a talk to the sailors.'

'Don't addle their English brains with your classical rubbish,' shouted Crispin satirically ; 'if you do, they may wreck us.'

'Wreck you!' said the Greek to himself, with a start. 'There is many a true word spoken in jest, my friend ; perhaps you may be wrecked before reaching Melnos.'

When Caliphronas had gone, Maurice relighted his pipe, which had gone out ; and, freed from the chattering of the Count, enjoyed the quiet beauty of the night, while Crispin hummed softly a ballad which Eunice used to sing,—

> *' Oh, winds and waves, oh, stars and sea,*
> *I would I were as blithe and free.'*

Above, the sky was almost of a purple colour in the sultry night, and the stars, brilliant and large, burned like lamps in the still air.   A serene moon, half veiled in fleecy clouds, arose above the chill snows of Taygetus, and a long glittering bridge of light extended from the land to the yacht.   The steady beat of the screw, which impelled the vessel through the silent waters, sounded in their ears, blending with the rich voice of Caliphronas, who had climbed up the mast, and was clinging to the weather rigging like a spectral figure in the shadowy glimmer of moon and star.

> '*The earth breathes fragrant breaths to-night,*
> *And the perfume blows from the land.*
> *Oh, I can see the waters kissing her shores,*
> *Even as I would kiss thee, my belovèd,*
> *With thy breath more fragrant than these languid scents*
> *Floating from the distant isles of rose-filled gardens.*'

'I wish I knew Greek,' said Maurice, as the Count paused for a moment; 'those snatches of song sound so beautiful.'

'They are beautiful,' replied Crispin idly; 'I have often thought of translating some of them into English.   Listen!

> '*I see Dione rising from the waters,*
> *A Venus of the moonlight night.*
> *Why wavest thou thy arms as ivory gleaming?*
> *Why do I see thine eyes flash as the evening star?*
> *Thy voice is as the murmur of breathing waves*
> *In twilight on a sandy beach.*
> *Callest thou me to thy home below?*
> *Ah, I will come, and beneath the placid waters*
> *Coldly white will I lie on thy cold white breast.*
> *But thro' the door of death must I pass to gain such blisses.*

''Tis like the lyrics of Callicles in Arnold's poem,' said Crispin, taking off his cap; 'stray fragments of song scattered by the winds.'

'Or like the songs in "Pippa Passes,"' suggested Maurice speculatively; 'but I am afraid the singing of Caliphronas will not do so much good as Pippa's.'

A long sigh floated past them on the still waters, like the melancholy cry of a bird, and died away sadly in the distance.

'Calypso sighing for Ulysses,' observed Crispin, without altering his position; 'though I daresay it is only the wind moaning through the ropes.'

'Let us think it is the voice calling, Pan is dead!'

'We are classical to - night. Caliphronas has inoculated us with his antique dreams. Well, when one is in fairyland, one must dream romances.'

'Suppose you tell me your romance,' said Maurice abruptly.

'Of my past life? Yes; I will do so; but you must promise to keep it secret.'

'I promise.'

'I am afraid you will think but little of it when you know all; but I promised to tell you, so I will now fulfil my promise. In the first place, you know my name is Crispin.'

'Yes; and have often wondered at its terseness. Have you no surname?'

'No legal surname.'

'Why not?'

'Because I am a natural son.'

'Illegitimate!' said Maurice, startled.

'Yes. Now you see the reason for my returning to Melnos.'

'You wish to find out who you really are.'

'I do; from Justinian.'

'But who is this mysterious Justinian?'

'And this equally mysterious Caliphronas, and Alcibiades, and Crispin. You are in a world of mystery here, and will see many things on Melnos which will excite your wonderment. But come, I will lift a portion of the veil, and place you in possession of facts which may be of use to you in the future.'

'I am all attention.'

Crispin settled himself more comfortably, and, fixing his earnest eyes upon Maurice, began his story without further remark.

'My first memories are of the island of Melnos, where I was *not* born. No; I was taken there with my mother when I was an infant; but the land of my birth I do not know. English I am, certainly; but for all I know, the ocean may have witnessed my coming into the world. As I grew up, I thought Justinian was my father, for my mother always led me to believe such was the case, and certainly he was very kind to me. This Justinian, of whom you have often heard me speak, is not a Greek, but an Englishman; but of his real name I am ignorant, nor do I know the reason that he lives in this island exile. Now you can see the reason I speak English so well, for from my earliest years I was brought up with the sound of it in my ears; so also was Caliphronas.'

'Is he related to Justinian?'

'No; nor was he born in Ithaca; nor is he a count; nor is his name Caliphronas. Count Constantine Caliphronas, better known in these waters as Andros, comes from the island of the name; and Justinian, struck by his beauty as a child, adopted him as a son, and brought him up with me. The English tongue we were both taught from our cradles; so you now know the reason we both speak it so well. In those early days I always thought Justinian was my father, and Caliphronas was my brother; but as I grew up I was undeceived on these points. My mother died when I was still a child, and I was therefore left to the sole guardianship of this pseudo-Englishman. As I told you, he rules over a kind of patriarchal community in this little-known island; and the life seems to suit him, for he is a kind of freebooter in his way, fierce and lawless, though years have now tamed his spirit to a considerable extent. Caliphronas, or rather Andros, and myself were brought up in a wild sort of fashion,—always in the open air, on the waters, fishing, riding, sailing, fighting '—

'Fighting!' cried Maurice in surprise.

'Yes. Oh, there are strange things in these Greek waters, I assure you! On an adjacent island lived a kind of semi-pirate called Alcibiades, who was, and is, a thorough blackguard. He used to cruise about in a small craft in order to levy blackmail on the inhabitants of the other islands, and in these cruises Andros and myself very often joined. There was no killing, you understand; but sometimes the peasants objected to be robbed, so there was often a fight, ending in broken heads.'

'But the law?'

'Oh, there is precious little law in these parts. Brigandism is not yet extinct, whatever you English may think. Besides, Alcibiades was a moderate sort of pirate, and was cunning enough not to go too far. He would rob a poor man of his last drachma, but he would not cut his throat. I don't think Justinian blamed him for this piratical existence; indeed, I think he rather envied his wild life, and, had he been young enough, would certainly have joined him in partnership. As it was, he allowed Andros and myself to form part of the band of Alcibiades, which we, wild, uncultured scamps as we were, regarded as a great privilege.'

'And how long did this buccaneering go on?'

'So far as I am concerned, for some years; but as regards Caliphronas, I daresay he is at it yet.'

'What! is he a thief?'

'Oh no; a thief is a vulgar thing. Caliphronas is

a picturesque freebooter, and simply plunders on a large scale. I've no doubt his visit to England was paid for out of his ill-gotten gains.'

' And is this Alcibiades still living?'

'Oh yes; you will see him, I have no doubt, for he is a great friend of Justinian's.'

' But who is this Justinian?'

Crispin paused for a moment and seemed to consider, then replied with great deliberation,—

'I can hardly tell you. He is an Englishman, so you must be content with knowing only that. Later on I may tell you something about him, but not now.'

'Well, and how did you escape from this piratical existence?'

'Oh, Caliphronas was the main cause of my leaving Melnos. After my mother died, I made several discoveries—one, that Andros was not my brother, as I had hitherto supposed; and another, that Justinian was not my father. Being a comparative child, I did not pay much attention to these facts; but when I was about eighteen years of age, I began to ask Justinian questions as to my parentage, but he refused to tell me.'

' Were you always called Crispin?'

' Yes, always. Justinian, in spite of his fierce, wild nature, has a vein of romance in him, and, as he arrived at Melnos with myself and my mother on St. Crispin's day, called me after that saint. My mother fell in with his humour, and from the time I landed at Melnos I was called nothing else but Crispin.'

'And how was Caliphronas responsible for your leaving Melnos?'

'Oh, it was a kind of Esau and Jacob business. I was Esau, and Andros Jacob, the favoured one. Justinian thought me rather a milksop, because I did not care about our piratical. excursions with Alcibiades, in which Caliphronas, born scamp as he was, delighted. At all events, Caliphronas, in order to curry favour with Justinian, and secure his own well-being, did his best to estrange us still further, and very soon my adopted father broke out into open hatred of me. One day, when I refused to join in one of Alcibiades' little trips in search of plunder, he taunted me with being a man of peace, like my father; and, when I demanded who my father was, refused to tell me anything more than that I was illegitimate. From words we came to blows, for both of us were very hot-tempered, and the end of it was that Justinian ordered me to leave the island, much to the delight of Caliphronas, who wanted to secure it to himself.'

'And you left Melnos?'

'Yes; I could not help myself, as Justinian had plenty of scoundrels to do his bidding; and, had he given the word, I have no doubt Alcibiades would have put a stone round my neck, and dropped me into the sea.'

'But, my dear Crispin, all this lawlessness now-a-days!'

Crispin shrugged his shoulders with a smile.

'My dear fellow, you gentlemen of England, who live at home in ease, do not know what lawlessness still exists in the East. To be sure, I speak of over ten years ago, and things are better now; still, I think a good many things go on in the vicinity of Melnos which Justice would scarcely approve of; but, so long as nothing very bad happens, why, she winks at small crimes. If I had been dropped into the sea, who would have been a bit the wiser? no one except the islanders, and they would not have troubled themselves over such a trifle, especially as I was not popular among them. Caliphronas, Justinian, and Alcibiades are all their divinities, not a poor poet like me, who shrinks from their scampish ways.'

'So you left Melnos in the end?'

'Yes; like the boy in the fairy tale, I went out

into the wide, wide world to seek my fortune. I managed to work my passage to Athens, and arrived there without even the traditional penny. Fortunately, I knew modern Greek and English thoroughly well, so was fortunate enough to obtain a situation as a corresponding clerk in a firm of merchants who traded with England, but I did not remain there long.'

'Where did you make all your money?'

'Ah, that is what I am now going to tell you. Fortune evidently wished to make reparation for having brought me into the world with a stigma on my name, so threw me into the way of a rich Englishman, whom I met at the house of my employer. He heard my story, and was much impressed with it; and then discovered that I had the talent to string verses together, and also a faculty for music. Being passionately fond of such things, he made up his mind that he had discovered a genius; and, being without a relative in the world, he adopted me as his son and made me his heir.'

'You seem to have passed your life in being adopted,' said Maurice, who was deeply interested in this romantic history.

'Only twice. First Justinian, then my English father. I need not tell you his name, as I did not take it, preferring to be called Crispin until such time

as I discovered my real parent. Well, my benefactor,
who was very learned, began to educate me, and also
placed me at school. I suppose I made good use of
my time, as I soon became sufficiently accomplished
to win his approval. We travelled all over the
Continent—a great deal in the East—until I was
about twenty-seven years of age, when he died at
Damascus, and left me heir to all his property,
amounting to some twelve thousand a year.'

'Fortunate man!'

'Yes; I thought I was too fortunate, and had some
compunction in taking so large an income, fearing
lest I might be robbing some relative of my benefactor, more entitled to it. When I buried my
adopted father at Damascus, I came to England
and saw his lawyers, who were quite satisfied with
my identity, owing to the papers which I produced.
The will, of course, was in their possession, as my
benefactor had returned to England when I was at
school, and made his will in my favour. The lawyers
told me that there were no relatives alive, and
that I was justly entitled to spend the money, so
that is how I became rich. The rest of my life you
know.'

'You published a volume of poems, became the
mystery of London, saw Eunice, fell in love with

her, and came down to the Grange—yes, I know all that; but have you made no effort to discover who you are?'

'Yes. I went to Melnos three years ago and saw Justinian, but he refused to help me in any way; so I returned to England in despair. Now, however, I am going back with certain knowledge of Justinian's past life, which I will make use of to force him to tell me what I wish to know.'

'You don't believe his story about your illegitimacy?'

'No. If I can get the truth out of him, I believe I shall find I have a right to a legal surname, and I am anxious to establish this fact in order to marry Eunice. As it is, I cannot marry her without inflicting on her the disgrace I feel myself; besides, her mother would not consent to the marriage, nor would you.'

'My dear fellow, I am not so narrow-minded as all that.'

'Still, I know your English prejudices. You say that out of kindness, but if your cousin marries, you would prefer her husband to have a spotless name.'

'Certainly.'

'Then I am going to make Justinian give me one. I know, if he tells the truth, I shall discover I have been born in wedlock. Of his own free will he refuses

to tell me ; now, however, owing to my knowledge of
his past, I can force his confidence.'

'And what about Helena ? '

'She is Justinian's daughter. There is no stain on
her birth ; so if you love her, as I am sure you will,
you can marry her without fear.'

'Her father seems rather a terrible old person.'

'He is a scamp, I am afraid. Still, he is a man
of good family.'

'How do you know ? '

'I have made certain discoveries while in England,
and now know more about Justinian than he thinks.'

'Is Helena as charming as she looks ? ' asked
Maurice anxiously.

'Yes,' replied Crispin emphatically. 'She is a pure,
good woman, and will make you an excellent wife ;
but you have a rival.'

'Alcibiades ? '

'No ; Caliphronas.'

'I thought as much,' said Maurice, with a start,
remembering the Greek's jealousy concerning the
portrait. 'But if he loves Helena, why did he show
me her picture, which has been my sole reason for
this journey.'

'Wheels within wheels ! ' replied Crispin significantly.

'More mystery?'

'Yes; there are still some things for you to learn, but I cannot tell you of them now, as I have made a promise.'

'To whom?'

'Caliphronas.'

'Caliphronas!' cried that gentleman, who had approached them quietly; 'and what are you saying about Caliphronas?'

'A good many things,' said Crispin rapidly, in Greek. 'I have been telling him who I am.'

The Greek flushed with rage, and then laughed.

'That is your business, but I trust you did not break faith?'

'About Justinian, no; about Helena, no; but I have told him all your early life.'

Caliphronas made a dart at Crispin with uplifted hand, but Maurice sprang up and caught him in his arms, where he writhed like an eel.

'Traitor!' he hissed in Greek; 'traitor!'

END OF VOL. I.

MORRISON AND GIBB, PRINTERS, EDINBURGH

www.ingramcontent.com/pod-product-compliance
Lightning Source LLC
Chambersburg PA
CBHW020902020726
47497CB00005B/1521